THE
Match
MAKER

THE Match MAKER

KAREY WHITE

ORANGE DOOR PRESS

ISBN: 978-1-941898-02-4
Published by Orange Door Press

For Leslie,
It's coming!
I'm sure of it

A perfect match
I love you

Other Books by Karey White

Gifted

For What It's Worth

My Own Mr. Darcy

Maggie's Song
(From the Timeless Romance Anthology: Love
Letters Collection)

Lost and Found
(A Ripple Effect Romance Novella)

The Husband Maker (The Husband Maker, Book 1)

Chapter 1

You'd think as many times as I had gone through this, I would have been prepared. Just like Martha Stewart can whip together a pound cake with her eyes closed, I should be able to work through my husband maker routine with a minimal recipe. Take one Charlotte. Add one man. Date. Break up. Count the weeks until he's engaged. (Except for Jered. With Jered I only had to count the days—eleven, in case you're curious.) Watch man get married. Repeat.

It was almost as simple as the instructions on a shampoo bottle. In theory. In practice, not so much.

I had been through minor variations of this recipe more than a dozen times in the last nine years. Fourteen if I counted Kyle. And why wouldn't I count him? Although we hadn't made it to the engagement stage, he was probably the most serious relationship I had ever had. We'd loved each other.

I still loved him.

I wanted to rewind the day and not come back to Jayne's office. If I could return to lunch, I could step in a manhole on my way to my car and break my leg. A trip to the emergency room and six weeks on crutches was far preferable to the look of pity on Jayne's face. A week in traction would hurt less than finding out Kyle was engaged.

Sadly, I wasn't in the emergency room. I had come back to the office, sat across from a teary Jayne, and learned Kyle was getting married. In a shell-shocked state, I had returned to my desk and foolishly entered the words "Kyle Aldsworth engaged" under an arrangement of spring flowers that spelled "Google." There was no going back. I'd seen the photograph.

Even though we'd been apart for six months, I had loved Kyle every single day. If Cupid put me under oath in his courtroom of love, I would have to admit that there have been many times since we broke up when I've brought up his number (and his handsome face) on my phone and debated with myself whether or not I should call him. I've so desperately wanted to hear his voice that sometimes I've brushed my thumb over the call button, tempting fate to let me "accidentally" make the call. I've typed out at least a dozen texts telling him I made a mistake and I would do my best to be a good politician's wife.

I've never sent them.

I've looked through the pictures on my phone hundreds of times—Kyle's furrowed brow as he concentrated on making a perfect cheese ball, his athletic body jumping the wake behind the boat, the silly face he had made to try to get me to snort, and my favorite, Kyle sitting in the great room at Lake Tahoe. He was laughing at something his dad had said and I had the perfect angle to capture his laugh-lines, his interesting nose, and of course that smile.

If anyone knew how many times I had looked at that picture in the last six months, they would probably have staged an intervention. About a month ago, I'd misplaced my phone. I tore the apartment to pieces before I finally found it in the bottom of the hamper. All I had thought about as I searched was that photograph. Not the pages of notes I kept on my phone for upcoming jobs or my dozens of contacts. Just that picture. When I found my phone, I emailed myself the photographs of Kyle. I didn't want to risk losing them again.

I've imagined Kyle doing the same thing. I've pictured him pining over me, punching in my number and almost calling me, looking at pictures and wishing we hadn't parted ways.

My heart has wanted us to get back together. If only my stupid head could figure out a way to make it work.

But now it didn't matter. Kyle was engaged, which meant he hadn't spent the last six months longing for me. He had probably deleted the photographic evidence that we had been in love. Maybe he'd even removed my number from his phone.

For a few seconds, I let myself be angry with my best friend, Angus. I knew that was a completely irrational response, but if he were still dating Wyatt, Kyle wouldn't be engaged to her.

Yes, it's Wyatt, but you probably already figured that out. I shouldn't be surprised. They're perfect for each other. And I don't mean that in a snarky, Miley Cyrus and Justin Beiber deserve each other kind of way. Kyle and Wyatt are really, truly perfect for each other.

I looked back at the image on my computer. The photographer had captured them walking down the sidewalk, arm in arm, looking at each other and laughing. Wyatt's wavy, red hair was swinging playfully and Kyle's hair was . . . Kyle's hair. Wyatt wore a flowing navy dress and looked like a supermodel, but that wasn't what I couldn't look away from. It was their eyes that squeezed my heart so hard it was a miracle it kept beating. Wyatt looked enchanted by what Kyle had just said and Kyle looked like he wanted to eat Wyatt for dessert. What more was there to say? The photograph could have been the movie poster for a romantic comedy. In fact, a casting director would have won an Oscar for casting these two opposite each other.

It was more than I could take.

I exited the story and pulled up my email.

To: jayne@jaynefife.com

From: ce@jaynefife.com

Time: 1:18 p.m.

SUBJECT: Can I go home?

Hey, Jayne. Do you mind if I call it a day? I've got the Adventureland Theme Park map I can work on from home.

Less than a minute later, Jayne emailed back.

To: ce@jaynefife.com

From: jayne@jaynefife.com

Time: 1:19

Re: Can I go home?

Of course you can. Please call me if I can do anything.

Charlotte, I'm so sorry. You have no idea.

I'd say have a good weekend, but I doubt you will. Please try though. I'll see you Monday.

To: jayne@jaynefife.com

From: ce@jaynefife.com

Time: 1:20 p.m.

RE: Can I go home?

Don't be sorry. You didn't do anything wrong. Don't worry about me. I'm fine.

I swallowed hard and fixed what I hoped was a normal expression on my face. I closed my office door and walked to the elevator, careful not to look in Jayne's office. If she tried to comfort me anymore, I'd lose it, and that would make her feel even worse.

The elevator door opened and Keith stepped out. Great!

"Hey, Charlotte?" The smile left his face when he saw me, and his voice took on a tone of concern. "Are you okay?"

"Oh yeah. Just starting my weekend a little early."

Keith studied my face. I could tell he wasn't buying it, but thankfully, he let it slide. "Lucky you. See you Monday."

He watched my fake smile until the elevator doors closed. I collapsed into the corner. I tried not to cry, but all my bleary eyes could see was the movie poster I had created in my mind. "His First Lady" starring Kyle Aldsworth and Wyatt . . . Surely I'd heard Wyatt's last name, but if I had, I couldn't remember it. "His First Lady" starring Kyle Aldsworth and Wyatt Man Stealer.

Now that was snarky, and I immediately felt bad for thinking it. A person can't steal something from you if you've already given it away.

Suddenly, like the storming of Normandy, the tears came.

Chapter 2

I spent the weekend in my room. I came out long enough to eat four Toaster Strudels on Saturday and a Cup O'Noodles on Sunday.

Mia, my roommate, accepted my request that I be allowed to work undisturbed all weekend, even though she gave me a strange look and knocked on the door to ask if I was okay several times. I ignored phone calls from Jayne and my sister, McKayla. I would see Jayne on Monday and if it was important, McKayla would call again. Sunday evening, I ignored Aleena's first three phone calls, but when my phone vibrated for the fourth time, I decided something might be wrong and picked up.

"Where are you and why aren't you answering your phone?" Aleena said.

"I'm at home." I ignored the second part of her question.

"Are you coming?" I could hear voices and music in the background.

"Coming where?"

Aleena sighed. "Really, Charlotte?"

I slogged through my swampy brain trying to figure out what I had forgotten. And then it hit me like David's stone hitting Goliath, and I fell back on my bed from the force of it.

"Oh no. Aleena, I'm so sorry. I'm a horrible friend."

"You can say that again. What are you doing that's so important you forgot my birthday?"

Aleena's dad had closed his Chinese restaurant and was having a huge party for Aleena's twenty-fifth birthday. She had made me promise weeks ago that I'd be there to help her get through the inevitable barrage of arranged dates her family and friends would try to push on her since she was rapidly turning into an old maid. And I had let her down. "I'm so sorry. I have your present here and everything."

"Then get over here." Her voice became muffled and quiet. "This is worse than I thought. Everyone my parents know is trying to marry me off to someone. Dad's accountant even suggested I go out with his brother. He's at least fifty."

I looked down at the pajamas I had been wearing for the better part of three days and sniffed my armpit. There was no way I could go anywhere without a full-on scouring. "I'm sorry, Aleena. I can't. It's been a horrible weekend. I promise I'll make it up to you."

Aleena didn't respond right away, and I felt worse by the second. "What did you get me?" she finally asked, and I could tell she was trying to cover up her hurt feelings.

"Something you're going to love. I promise."

Again there was a long pause. "Good. I'll swing by after the party and pick it up."

"Or I can bring it by the restaurant tomorrow." If she was coming, I would have to fumigate my room and take a shower tonight, and I wasn't sure I was up to the task.

"Nope. I'll be by about eleven."

Time to exorcise the stinky sloth and become a woman again.

I showered, dried my hair, and put on clean sweatpants and a t-shirt. I shoved my pajamas into the hamper and generously sprayed disinfectant inside and around the basket. I picked up two boxes worth of tissues I'd used and tossed to the floor over the past two days. I closed the thirteen tabs that each had a picture or article about Kyle and Wyatt, and I opened the Adventureland project I hadn't even thought about. Not that Aleena would know the difference, but it would be good if I could honestly tell Jayne I had looked at it over the weekend.

The only thing I couldn't remedy was my face. My eyes were red and puffy and my complexion splotchy. My Rudolph nose was actually peeling from wiping it so many times. I really should invest in tissues with lotion before my next heartbreak. Makeup only helped a little. Oh well. I would probably end up telling Aleena the truth anyway.

I smiled when I opened the door just after eleven.

Aleena cocked her head to the side and looked me up and down. "You look horrible."

"Gee, thanks. You look beautiful." She really did. Her hair was up, showing off her high cheekbones. Her knee-length dress had a full skirt and looked like blue delft China, matching her unusual blue eyes.

"I know I look good tonight. It was my party. I want to know why you look so awful. What's wrong?"

"I thought you were here to get your present?" I pulled Aleena into my bedroom and sat her on the end of the bed. Then I handed her the wrapped box I had pulled out of the closet.

"I'm not opening this until you tell me what's wrong. Are you sick?"

"No. Not unless you mean heartsick." I laughed, trying to pass it all off as a joke, but Aleena didn't join me. I plunked myself down on the bed and pulled my feet up under me. "Fine. You'll find out anyway." I took a deep breath. "Kyle's engaged."

Aleena shook her head. "I knew it."

"You did?" I asked.

"I was trying to figure out what would be so horrible that would make you forget my birthday, and I thought it must have something to do with Kyle."

I sighed. "I'm pathetic."

Aleena looked sad but didn't disagree with my assessment. "I told you the other day, Charlotte. It's time to move on. Do you believe me now?"

I shrugged.

"Charlotte, you can't just sit here and wallow."

"Why not? I've wallowed all weekend and look how great I am." I tried to laugh again, but it came out as a sad, little sob.

Aleena reached out and patted my leg. "Wallowing isn't working for you. You really look dreadful." She continued to pat my leg as she thought. "I'm taking over your love life for you."

"Don't be an idiot."

"I'm not. I opened a fortune cookie tonight and I think it was supposed to be yours."

I rolled my eyes. "If you opened a fortune cookie tonight, it's yours."

"I'm giving it to you."

"I don't think that's how it's supposed to work," I said.

Aleena waved me away and let out a little puff of air between her lips. "My fortune. My rules. Want to know what it said?"

I bit. "Fine. What did it say?"

"Romance will come to you from foreign lands."

"You're totally making that up."

Aleena grabbed her clutch and started digging through it. "Why do you always doubt me? I promise that's what it said."

"Not to be mean, but you should keep any fortune that's about romance. You're in the same boat I am."

"That's not true. I'm in a happy boat. It's yellow and has flowers painted on the side. You're in a gray boat that's taking on water. You need my fortune more than I do. Aha!" She handed me a folded strip of paper.

I unfolded it and read the tiny words aloud. "Romance will come to you from foreign lands." I tried to hand it back to her.

"No, you keep it. Look at you. You need it more than I do. Besides, you said you had a friend you'd set me up with, so I'll help arrange a date for you with the foreigner and you can set me up with your friend."

I cringed. I had told Aleena I would set up a blind date with Angus months ago. I really was a horrible friend. I needed to make that happen sooner than later. Maybe this week.

"So how do I find this true love?"

"Forget true love. It says romance. And we just met someone from a foreign land that I could have sworn was interested in you."

On Friday, Aleena and I had gone to lunch at Imperial Palace. While there, we had met Flynn and Bruce, two brothers from Scotland. Bruce was now living in San Francisco and working at an architecture firm. Flynn was in town visiting. They were both handsome and had seemed nice. Aleena was sure Flynn had flirted with me. I wasn't ready to return the interest.

"So you want me to troll the streets looking for the Scotsman?"

"Nope. I'm going to call his brother's office tomorrow and get his number for you. And then you're going to call him and let that nice, foreign Paul Bunyan help you rebound. You're going to have fun. You're going to enjoy his accent. You're going to laugh. And you're going to stop thinking about Kyle."

I shook my head. "I'll look desperate."

She scowled at me. "No you won't. You'll look friendly."

I shook my head more emphatically.

"Stop it, Charlotte. I'm your friend, so I'm going to be honest with you. You *are* desperate, whether you want to admit it or not. So let's get you out of your rut and you can go enjoy that cute Scotsman's company."

"I don't feel like dating anyone," I whispered.

Aleena's voice turned sympathetic. "Which is exactly why you need to. You're young and beautiful and fun and you've grieved long enough. It's time. Okay?"

I didn't answer.

"Say okay so I can open my present. Please?"

I smiled a little. "Okay. Now open your present. You're going to love them."

"Them?" Aleena said as she ripped off the wrapping paper. "Are you serious?" She pulled out the t-strap, green wedges.

"I hope I got the right size."

Aleena looked at the size and then held them to her chest. "Sevens. Exactly right. I love them." She hugged me with a shoe in each hand. "You know me so well."

I hugged her back. "Am I forgiven for being the worst friend alive and missing your party tonight?"

"Only if you're a willing tour guide for the Scot and if you set me up with your friend."

"You drive a hard bargain, girl."

"I know. My father would be so proud. But seriously, Charlotte. The men they were trying to pawn me off on." She gave me a horrified look.

"All right. If you track him down, I'll offer to take him sight-seeing."

I'd had trouble falling asleep all weekend, but this night it was more complicated. I was still hurting because of Kyle's upcoming nuptials, but now I had added a healthy (or unhealthy) dose of nerves. Had I really agreed to contact a stranger and offer to be his San Francisco tour guide? I wasn't in the mood to get out of bed, let alone point out the sites and make small talk. Maybe Aleena wouldn't remember the name of Bruce's architecture firm. Maybe Bruce's brother, Flynn, would have already returned to the Isle of handsome lumberjacks with lots of freckles.

I was recalling those fascinating freckles and that charming smile when I realized something alarming. Aleena was right. It was time for me to pull myself out of the Kyle quicksand that had me trapped. When Kyle and I had parted, I had decided to take some time away from dating to heal and regroup, but instead, I'd pined and second-guessed myself. This six months hadn't been good for me, and as much as I wanted to park myself in the junkyard of broken hearts, I knew it was time to get this old clunker a tune-up and take her out for a spin.

I thought about Kyle and Wyatt, and it knocked the wind out of me for a minute, but I loved Kyle and wanted him to be happy. As much as I hated to admit it, Kyle was making a good choice. I liked Wyatt and there was no doubt she was a good fit for his life. Much better than I ever could have been. It was time to wish them well and move on.

And why not move on with a handsome, Scottish man with a beautiful accent and a charming smile? It might be nice to date someone with no pressure. After all, he would be heading back to Scotland, so this could be short, fun, and easy. A little rebound fling. Maybe Flynn really could help take my mind off Kyle.

Chapter 3

I read the message again.

Aleena: His name is Flynn, but you probably remember that. He's in town until Sunday night. (That doesn't mean you can put this off. I'll be checking in on you at three to see if you've called him.) He can be reached at 415-555-9806. Bruce said he'll be excited to hear from you. wink wink CALL HIM NOW!!!

I looked at the time. Two forty-six. I'd been putting this off for almost two hours and now I had fourteen minutes before Aleena checked in. Knowing Aleena, I probably had more like ten minutes.

I bit my lip and dialed the number.

"Hello."

I smiled. I couldn't help it. Aleena was right. His accent was beautiful.

"Hi. This is Charlotte. I don't know if you remember who I am—"

"Course I do. I've been expecting your call."

"You have?"

"Bruce rang and told me ya might be callin'. I've been

14

waitin'. And hopin'."

"And I've been sitting here for the last two hours worrying about this."

Flynn laughed. "Nothin' to worry about. I'm not scary."

"That's debatable."

Flynn laughed again. "Was it the accent scared ya?"

"No, the accent's fine."

"It's because of *Braveheart*? I promise we're not all blue-painted warriors."

"*Braveheart* doesn't scare me either."

"Then what's to be afraid of?"

Maybe it was the laughter in his voice or that I'd never see him again in a week's time. Whatever it was, I felt strangely free to say what I was thinking. "You're a man."

"You're afraid of men?"

I took a deep breath. This wasn't going the way I expected. "I'm just coming off a hard breakup, so men in general make me skittish."

"Ah. Well, ya don't need to fret. I'm a nice guy."

"Good to know."

"If I'd had your number, Charlotte, I would have called you."

My name had never sounded so good. I wanted to ask him to say it again, but thought better of it.

"Really?"

"Aye. Bruce was supposed to show me around, but his boss handed him a project he can't put off, and you and your friend are the only other people I know."

"That's pretty sad for you since you don't really

know us."

"True, but ya have jovial eyes and a pleasing smile, so I knew we'd be friends right off."

No one has ever told me I have jovial eyes. The phrase was sweet, and I felt some of my nerves scamper away.

"Charlotte? You still there?" It was like my name had been created to be spoken with a Scottish accent.

"I'm here."

"Did ya call with something specific in mind or can I ask you out?"

Flynn kept catching me off guard. "Uh, well, I had something in mind, but if you'd like to ask me out, go right ahead."

"Brilliant. Bruce got tickets for a tour of Alcatraz, but he can't go. Would you like to go with me? That is, if you're available. They're for tomorrow morning. Nine-forty."

"I'm supposed to work."

"Ah, of course ya are. It was too much ta hope for."

"But I can probably get it off. I have a ton of vacation time saved up."

"You don't mind spending your vacation on someone ya don't even know?"

"I haven't been to Alcatraz since we went there for a seventh grade field trip. It sounds like fun."

We made arrangements to meet at Pier 33.

"Thanks for calling, Charlotte. Even though you were scared. Ya must be a brave girl."

Right now I wasn't sure if I was brave or foolish. I guess I'd find out tomorrow.

I called Jayne and arranged to take the day off. I had nearly three weeks of vacation days saved up, but even if I hadn't, Jayne would probably have paid me to take the day off, just to ease her guilty conscience.

"Please tell me you're not going to sit at home crying," she said after she had agreed to the time off.

"Actually, I need the day off because I have a date."

"Oh, that's wonderful." The relief in her voice made me realize how terrible she had been feeling. "Who are you going out with?"

"A handsome tourist from Scotland."

"Ooh, sounds romantic."

"It's not. It's just a friendly trip to Alcatraz. His brother can't go with him and it wouldn't be much fun for him to go alone."

"Oh." Jayne sounded disappointed. "Well, have fun, and if you need any more time off, I'm sure we can arrange it."

My cell phone buzzed almost before I had hung up the office phone.

Aleena: Did you call him?

Me: I'm going to Alcatraz with him tomorrow.

Aleena: Yay! I don't mean to pester you, but I told Doug (Dad's accountant) that I'm dating your friend. It was the only way he'd leave me alone. He brought in a picture of his brother today and not only is he at least 50, I'm positive he was wearing a toupee. I had to put a stop to his match making. I feel guilty for lying, so I need you to set me up. Even if it's just for lunch.

Me: I'm on it. I'll have a date set up by the end of the day. Sorry I'm such a slacker.

Aleena: No problem. I just don't want to have to lie to him every time he stops by.

I hadn't seen Angus for almost two weeks. Did he even know about Wyatt and Kyle? I sent him a text.

Me: I think we need Luigi's.

Luigi's was our long-standing eatery when we needed therapy—not legitimate, professional counselling, but the consoling that comes from commiserating over food with a good friend. It was more an excuse to get together and help each other through the hard times in our dating lives.

Angus didn't answer right away. In fact, I had sketched out a postcard for Adventureland by the time he responded half an hour later.

Angus: I didn't know you were dating anyone.

Me: I haven't been. But I think I'm ready to test the dating waters again. Sort of. Something safe and friendly and less stressful. If you know what I mean. BTW, are you dating anyone?

Angus: No. Just putting in long hours at work.

Me: Good. Not about the long hours. Good that you're not dating someone.

Angus: Why is that good?

Me: Well, I kinda want to talk to you in person, 'cause I think I've got the perfect girl for you to date.

Angus: Oh really? And who might that be?

Me: That is, if you have time to date.

Angus: Charles, I've always had time for the right girl.

Me: Good, because I think this might be the girl you've been waiting for. Someone you probably should have dated a long time ago. I think. I hope. Let's go to Luigi's and I'll tell you all about her?

Angus: Have you been talking to Will?

Me: Yeah.

Angus: About me and dating?

Me: Of course. Along with many other subjects.

Angus: Do I dare ask what he said about me?

Me: You can always ask, but that doesn't mean I'll tell. Seriously though, most of the time we talk about Emily. I wish they would just go out of town and let me babysit that girl for days.

Angus: I saw her Saturday. I can't believe how much she's grown.

Me: I know. She'll be starting school before we know it.

Angus: She called me Uncle Angus. I'm pretty sure those were her first words.

Me: Wow. That's pretty impressive for a 3 month old.

Angus: I guess I'm just her favorite.

Me: You can't make me jealous. At least not where Emily is concerned. I'm pretty sure she's going to love me the most.

Angus: You're probably right. Doesn't everyone love you most?

Me: We seem to have gotten sidetracked. When can you meet for therapy?

Angus: As luck would have it, I'm finishing a shift at 6 tonight.

Me: Will you be too tired? How long have you been on?

Angus: It was a 24 hr shift, but I took two naps. I don't work again until tomorrow night. Let's go tonight.

Me: If you're sure.

Angus: I'm sure. Pick you up at 8?

Me: 8 it is.

"When did you go getting all stylish?" I asked when I got in Angus's car.

"I figured it was time to invest in a few things other than jeans and sweatshirts now that I get a paycheck."

"You look nice. I haven't seen you in cords since, what, fourth grade?"

I reached over and ran my hand over the brown corduroy pants he wore with a button-down shirt and a pale blue cardigan straight out of Mr. Rogers' closet.

"Did I have cords in fourth grade? I don't remember ever owning a pair before."

"You and Will both had a pair of navy blue corduroy pants. You used to call each other to be sure you were wearing them on the same day."

"Were those cords?"

"Yep."

"That seems like a girly thing to remember." The right side of his mouth quirked up.

"I guess that's why I can remember and you can't."

"Well, you always look nice, so I figured I should make a little effort."

For a guy who had worked twenty-four hours

straight, Angus seemed pretty happy. I wondered if my news about Kyle and Wyatt would bring him down. I didn't say anything about their engagement on the way to Luigi's. We just caught up on the latest with work and his dad's improving health.

We ordered right after we were seated. We didn't need to see a menu since we always ordered the same thing. When the waitress had walked away, Angus leaned back in the booth. He looked good—happy and relaxed. His light brown hair looked like it had been cut recently, but even short, it managed to be a little messy. His smile reached his warm brown eyes and I almost didn't want to bring up Kyle and Wyatt and risk removing it from his cute face.

"You sure seem happy," I said.

"I am. I'm off for the next twenty-four hours and I'm hungry and ribs sound great, and we're actually here more for fun than for therapy."

"Well, there's a little therapy involved, but mostly it's because I think we both need to move on. I'm tired of moping around and I hope you are too. And of course, we might as well talk about all this stuff while we eat ribs and pie."

"Might as well. I'm glad you invited me. It's been awhile since we ate here."

"I know. Six months."

Angus grinned at me and I couldn't contain my smile. We sat there stupidly smirking at each other for several seconds. "I'm ready to hear whatever you have to tell me, so go ahead whenever."

Angus was so happy. Was it because he trusted me to

set him up with someone good and he was ready to start dating again? His cheerfulness made me excited to tell him about Aleena and a little flattered, too. He must trust me that I would only set him up with someone great, and I knew he wouldn't be disappointed by Aleena. She was smart, funny and gorgeous. I should have done this a lot sooner. Just because I'd been on a dating hiatus didn't mean Angus had to be.

But first, I needed to tell him about Kyle and Wyatt. He deserved to know, and I didn't want it to seem like I was keeping it from him. He would probably think it was because I was devastated—which I had been—but I didn't want Angus to worry about me. He'd probably be relieved to know I was through nursing my broken heart. He would be happy to know I was ready to start dating again.

Angus was still smiling. His eyes hadn't left my face.

I took a sip of water. "I have a lot I want to tell you tonight."

"I'm ready to hear it all."

"Okay. Do you want the good news or the bad news first?"

Angus's smile faltered a little. "There's bad news?"

"Well, yeah. Sort of. At least I thought it was bad news the first time I heard it. But honestly, the more I think about it, I don't feel like it's so bad. It makes sense and it somehow seems right, even though at first I was thrown for a loop. I just don't want it to upset you."

"Sounds complicated. I guess we might as well get the bad news out of the way first then."

Angus's hands were folded on the table in front of him. I reached out and put my hand on his wrist, hoping it would soften the blow of what I was about to say.

I took a deep breath. "Did you know Kyle and Wyatt are engaged?"

Angus's mouth dropped open for a moment before he recovered and closed it. "Seriously?"

I nodded.

"To each other?"

I nodded again.

We were quiet for several moments while the news sank in. Then Angus sat up a little straighter and put his hand over mine. "Are you okay?"

I nodded again. "I was surprised, and I spent a few days crying when I found out, but honestly, they make sense together. Don't you think?"

Angus's nod was almost imperceptible. "Yeah. They really do. Talk about a power couple."

"I know. They're perfect for each other. She's much better for Kyle than I ever could have been."

"I don't know about that," Angus said.

"I do. And you do too. You just don't want to hurt my feelings."

Angus squeezed my hand. "I'm happy for them. As long as you're okay."

I took a deep breath. "I'm going to be fine. I'm moving on."

"And apparently so am I." Angus was smiling again.

"Yes, you are," I said.

We moved our hands out of the way as the waitress put plates of ribs and coleslaw and baked beans on the table.

We dished up our plates and started eating. "So you

want to elaborate on how we're moving on?" Angus said between bites of ribs.

I swallowed and wiped my mouth on my napkin. "I've decided I need to get out again. I've been taking a break since Kyle, and all I've done for six months is feel bad and wish we were back together. It's probably good they're engaged, because now I know I need to stop wasting my time and I need to move on. I need to have some fun again. So tomorrow I'm going out on my first date in more than six months. With a guy from Scotland."

Angus's fork full of coleslaw froze on the way to his mouth.

"His name is Flynn," I said, "and he seems like a really nice guy. It'll give me a chance to go out and have some fun without it being a big thing. How serious can it be with a guy who lives halfway around the world, right?"

Angus's bite of coleslaw finally made it to his mouth and he chewed it slowly. When he swallowed, he spoke. "So . . . where exactly do I fit into this 'moving on' plan of yours?"

"I'm sure you've heard me talk about my friend Aleena. I want you to take her out. I think you two might really hit it off. You're both smart and funny and you're my best friends. You're going to love her. And she'll adore you."

I took a bite of beans and Angus took a bite of ribs. I wanted to know what he thought of the idea, but every time I thought he might say something, he took another bite of food. After four or five bites, I couldn't wait any longer. "Will you go out with her?"

Something had changed. Angus was no longer

smiling. His mood had become serious, and he was so intent on his food I wondered if he had heard me.

"Angus?"

His eyes met mine. "You really want me to take her out? What did you say her name was?"

"Aleena Li. You've heard me talk about her before, right?"

Angus nodded.

"I know you'll like her. She's awesome."

"What makes you think she'll like me?"

"Don't be silly. How could she not? You're the best guy out there. She would be crazy not to fall madly in love with you." What had happened to Angus's merry mood? Did he hate setups this much? Was he upset that I wanted to arrange a blind date for him?

Angus didn't look at me when he spoke. "If you really want me to go out with her, I will."

"Whew! You had me scared for a minute. I've told Aleena all about you, and if you'd have said no I don't know what I would have told her."

"Give me her number and I'll give her a call."

"Thank you, Angus. Once you get to know her, you'll be thanking me. I promise. Maybe we could double date sometime. That would be fun."

"No," Angus said shaking his head.

"Why not?" His hasty refusal surprised me. He shrugged and took another bite of food, but didn't answer.

When he finally swallowed, he changed the subject. "So what is this guy like? The tourist?"

I told Angus about how we had met Flynn and his brother at Imperial Palace, and how Aleena had helped them order their lunch. I told him about how Aleena had tracked down his number and how we had made plans to go to Alcatraz. "I'm more excited than I thought I would be," I said. "He seems like a really nice guy and I could listen to his accent for days. And it'll be safe. Since he's only here for about a week, it can just be casual and fun and no pressure."

As Angus drove me home, I saved Aleena's number in his phone. "You can come up for a while if you want," I said when we reached my street. "We could watch a movie or something."

"Thanks, but I'm pretty beat."

Of course he was. He had been working for twenty-four hours straight and then had come to dinner with me. No wonder he'd been so quiet. His exhaustion had probably caught up with him.

"I understand. Thanks for coming tonight. It was nice to spend some time together. Get a good night's sleep and text me when you call Aleena. I can't wait to see what you think of her."

I leaned across the car and hugged Angus.

"Bye, Charlotte," he said as I closed the car door. It wasn't until I was in my apartment that I realized he hadn't called me a nickname.

Chapter 4

I was sitting on a bench outside Pier 33 watching a
family from Boston. At least I think they were from
Boston. The father and mother were wearing Boston
College sweatshirts and their teenage son was in a vintage
Larry Bird Celtics jersey. Then they spoke and all doubt
about where they were from vanished.

"I wanted to take the night tour," the son said. "It
looks way cooler."

"The night tour was booked," said the father.

"We're lucky we got on a tour at all. And you'd better
enjoy this," said the mom. She handed a granola bar to her
son. "These tickets weren't cheap."

"Mom, you know I hate those things. They just make
me thirsty." The boy dropped the food in his mother's
bag.

I wished she would offer me the granola bar. I was
starving. I had gotten up in plenty of time, but I'd gone
through half my closet trying on different outfits. I knew
I was acting crazy, but I wanted to be sure my clothes
didn't send the wrong message. Of course I wanted to look

nice, but I didn't want to look like I was trying too hard. Coming up with a comfortable, reasonably cute ensemble that didn't give off an "I'm trying to look good for you" vibe was harder than I had expected. I finally settled on a flowered, coral dress and flat, brown sandals, but by that time, I had sacrificed breakfast.

So here I was, watching a sullen boy turn down a granola bar while my stomach rumbled. I looked at my cell phone. Did I have time to grab a snack before Flynn arrived?

The tall, attractive man that turned the corner, let me know I didn't have time. What was so appealing about him? He wasn't conventionally handsome. He certainly didn't have the movie star politician looks that Kyle has, but there was something about Flynn that grabbed my eyes and wouldn't let them go and that stirred my curiosity in a way it hadn't been stirred in some time.

This wasn't a date. It wasn't. This was just a step on my road to recovery.

I rolled my eyes at my silly melodrama.

Flynn smiled when he saw me and held up a bag in greeting. When he got a little closer, I saw it was from Noah's bagels. "I brought food."

"How did you know I was starving?"

"I didn't. I just knew I was, but I didn't want to eat in front of ya."

I slid over and he sat down beside me.

"I've got sweet and savory. There's lox and cream cheese and there's a honey walnut. You choose."

"You really don't care?"

"Ladies first."

"Or we could split them."

"Brilliant."

We each tore a bagel in half. Mine was much more even than Flynn's. He tried to give me the larger portion of the lox bagel, but I took the smaller half instead.

Passengers were gathering at the gate so we ate our bagels in line. Flynn threw the bag and wrappers into a garbage can by the gate, reached into his shirt pocket for the tickets, and handed them to the man in a black national park vest.

"That hit the spot," I said after I swallowed my last bite. "Thank you."

"My pleasure." Flynn put his hand on the small of my back to guide me onto the boat ahead of him. I shouldn't have even noticed the gesture, since this wasn't really a date.

When I think about my seventh grade trip to Alcatraz, it's like an old-fashioned movie. In fact, the whole trip is a gray blur. The overcast sky was gray, a gray wind whipped my hair into my eyes and mouth, and the whole island, including the buildings, were various saturations of gray. The only other color I remember from that day is red. Jackson Duncan ran into a wall or a post or something and ended up with a bloody nose. In my memories, I see red blood seeping between Jackson's gray fingers and dripping on the gray concrete of the Broadway cell block.

Today it was as if San Francisco had painted the world with a box of Prismacolor markers. Every color was bright and bold and clamoring for attention. The sky was having a blue screaming match with the water. Our ferry boat had been freshly painted and was a blinding white with red trim that dared you not to notice it. It looked like the requirement for admission had been bright clothes. Everyone looked like they had dressed in the electric hues of a PBS children's show. Sorry, you're in gray or black or olive? That's not much fun. You'll have to take the next tour. This tour's assignment is to look like a box of crayons.

Even Flynn was drenched in color, from his auburn hair, to his blue eyes, to his cinnamon freckles. He wore a periwinkle and navy plaid shirt and jeans. He had shaved since I saw him in Chinatown, and then he hadn't shaved for a couple of days. It was a perfect amount of manliness on his face that was softened by the sunshine. His whiskers glistened a little and made me want to touch them, but I didn't.

Touching his stubbly chin would have been something you do on a date, and this wasn't a date. This was an appointment. Like a doctor's appointment or a job interview. I was here so Flynn wouldn't have to see Alcatraz alone, so Bruce's ticket wouldn't go to waste. I was here to ease myself back into socializing with members of the opposite sex. I was here to keep myself from becoming a sad, weepy hermit.

Aleena was calling Flynn my safe, rebound guy. I wasn't calling him anything. Except Flynn. And I wasn't calling this anything. Except not a date.

"What?" I asked when I realized Flynn was watching me. We were standing at the rail on the back of the boat. White foam split the deep blue water as the boat moved. The morning sun felt warm on my face.

"You look a little angry. Is something wrong?"

"I'm not angry. I was just thinking."

"Angry thoughts?"

I smiled. "No. Not angry thoughts."

"That's better." Flynn nodded toward my smile. "You're pretty when you smile. You were pretty when you were frowning, too, but this is better."

I smiled a little wider.

"What were you thinkin'?"

I shook my head. "You don't want to know."

Flynn raised an eyebrow. "Why wouldn't I want to know?"

I shrugged.

"Ah, so you're making me guess?"

"I doubt you could guess what I was thinking."

"Can I try?"

I laughed. "Sure, you can try."

"And you'll tell me if I'm right?"

I knew he would never guess what I was thinking, so what was the harm in him trying? "Sure. I'll tell you if you're right."

"Well, you're frownin' but you say you're not angry, so it must be something you're fretting over. Am I on the right path?"

I shrugged and nodded a little at the same time. "Keep going. This might be very enlightening."

Flynn kept his expression serious as he looked at me, but it was clear from his eyes that he was smiling. "You said you've just been heartbroken and maybe you're not sure you want to date yet."

I opened my eyes wide and Flynn bit back his smile.

"And here you are with me. And you're finding me endlessly fascinating and you're starting to wonder how you're going to spend the day with me without falling madly in love."

A laugh that sounded more like a snort escaped my mouth. Flynn was now grinning.

"How'd I do?" he asked.

"Pretty good. Until you got to the falling in love with you part. I was actually trying to figure out how to make sure you knew this wasn't a date date. If you know what I mean."

"You want me to know this is just a date, not a date date?"

"I'm thinking of it more like an appointment instead of a date." I couldn't believe I was saying this to him, but we were both smiling, and he didn't seem the least bit upset. I suddenly felt comfortable and calm. He had practically read my mind and now I didn't have to worry, because he knew exactly where my head was.

"An appointment, eh? Isn't that more like a haircut? Or a filling in a tooth?"

I laughed again. "Maybe appointment is a bad choice of words."

"Let's just call it a play date. Like kids. That way we can have fun with no worries, and if I feel like it, I can pull your hair—"at this point he tugged on my ponytail "—or wrestle you to the ground."

Now I raised both eyebrows.

"Ya know. Like kids do when they're playing."

"Okay, it's a play date," I agreed. "Not an appointment. But wrestling me to the ground is strictly forbidden. And you don't need to worry. I'm not ready to fall in love with anyone right now. Not even a cute guy with a great accent."

"Ah, she's fallin' already." He bumped against me with his shoulder and we both smiled as we leaned on the rail and looked back at the silvery city.

We spent more than three hours on the island. We took the audio tour, which didn't lend itself to easy conversation. It's hard to talk when you're both wearing headphones. We did exchange several looks of surprise or revulsion as we listened to the stories.

We stood in front of a cell as we listened to the narration. At the back of the cell was a vent that had been enlarged with spoons. On the bed was the form of a man with his head on the pillow. Three men had escaped through the vents. They had made paper mache heads with hair they had collected from the prison barber. No one had realized they were missing until the next morning, when one of the guards tried to wake up one of the inmates. He reached in the cell and hit the pillow and the paper mache head fell to the floor. They had built a raft with fifty rubber raincoats they had stolen. They were never heard from again.

I turned to advance to the next part of the tour, but Flynn took my arm, just below the elbow. His warm fingers startled me. I turned toward him and saw that he had paused the tour and had moved one side of his headphones off his ear. It sat on his head at an odd angle and I smiled. I paused my recording.

"Do you think they survived?"

"Kind of a cool story if they did. They probably

escaped to Scotland and built themselves a little hut."

"Ya think we live in huts?" Flynn moved his hand and pretended to look hurt. I pretended I hadn't noticed his touch.

"That's not what I meant. I'm sure you live in a perfectly lovely house. But you're not an escaped prisoner."

"Actually there are some huts on the Isle of Lewis. But most people don't live in 'em."

"I hate to think of them drowning out there in the cold water," I said.

"They risked that when they made their escape. And don't forget, they were criminals."

"They were bank robbers, not murderers."

"Aye. True." He turned toward the cell. "It's a good thing it wasn't me in there. I'd have never fit through that vent."

"Hopefully you'd have never robbed a bank." He raised his eyebrows and quirked the corner of his mouth, straightened his headphones, and with the lightest touch to my back—I really needed to stop noticing that—we moved on.

Flynn wanted to look around the gift shop when we finished the tour, which was fine with me. I always spend some time looking over the souvenirs. I rarely buy anything, but it's good research. I browsed through the postcards while Flynn looked at books. Most of the postcards were old photographs. Alcatraz wasn't exactly the right tourist stop for the kind of souvenir materials I usually made.

I was studying a wall map of the island when Flynn

came up beside me. I noticed that he left several inches between us.

"What did you find?" I asked, eyeing his bag.

"Books."

"You like to read?"

"All the time. There are some long, quiet nights in Stornoway. These'll keep me company." He held up the bag. "Interesting map?"

"I just like to see what they're selling." We started walking toward the door. "I make promotional materials and souvenirs for tourist sites."

"Ya do?" He stopped just before the door. "Have you made anything for Alcatraz?"

I shook my head. "No. I've never done anything for a national park. I think they have a team of people who design their souvenirs. I create things for theme parks and little out of the way places."

"What're you working on now?"

"Yesterday I was designing key chains, postcards and refrigerator magnets for Adventureland. It's an amusement park."

"That's a great career. You must be artistic."

The hill leading down to the return ferry was steep. A group of tourists that had just arrived on the island walked by.

I couldn't remember ever seeing a clearer day. There wasn't a speck of smog in the air. Everything looked bright and freshly washed. Instead of working hard to break through the San Francisco mists, the hot sun had nothing to burn off and instead focused its heat on us. I was grateful when a little breeze cooled my face.

"What do you do? For your career?"

"We have a little hardware store in Stornoway."

"We?" For a quick moment I wondered if he had a wife. Wouldn't that just be perfect if my rebound guy was married?

"My mum and me. It's all mine now, but mum takes care of it when I'm gone. Mum and Jessie. It was my dad's store, but when he died, I took it over. Bruce was already gone to school to be an architect, so it made sense."

"Is Jessie your sister?"

Flynn stopped. "Look at that view. It wasn't all bad for the prisoners if they got to look at this."

I looked across the water, trying to see it with the eyes of someone new, someone who hadn't seen the bay area from almost every angle. It really was beautiful. We quietly looked for a minute before we continued down the hill to the boat.

"Sorry, what did you ask?"

"I asked if Jessie is your sister."

"No. It's just Bruce and me. Jessie is a girl from Stornoway. She works for me in the store."

"I'll bet it was hard for your mom to have Bruce move to San Francisco."

"Aye, but it was. She made me promise I wouldn't come visit Bruce and decide to stay." Flynn's mouth quirked up in a mischievous smile. "She wouldn't be too happy to know I was having a play date with a pretty girl."

I felt my cheeks flush and hoped he thought it was from the warm day. I smacked his arm with the back of my hand. "See, we should have called it an appointment."

"Well, I think play date is more accurate, but maybe

I should use the word appointment when I tell her."

"Or you could not tell her at all since she's got nothing to worry about."

I could see Flynn's smile out of the corner of my eye, but I refused to make eye contact with him.

We looked through Flynn's books on the ferry ride back to San Francisco. He had purchased a book about the escape from Alcatraz, the biography of The Birdman of Alcatraz, and a book about the Indian Occupation of the island in the early seventies.

"They look interesting," I said.

"You haven't read any of them?"

I shook my head.

"I'll let you know what I think of them when I'm finished." A little warning bell went off. This was the first time he had said anything that would indicate contact after he left. Unless he planned to read them while he was here. That would be some fast reading, but not impossible.

We were almost to Pier 33 when I started worrying about what came next. I'd had a good time. A really good time. Flynn was charming and cute. That was the problem. I hadn't thought I would be enjoying myself this much. I wasn't supposed to be aware of our proximity every second. I shouldn't notice every time his arm accidentally brushed mine. I wasn't supposed to want to look at his face.

The safest thing would be for me to go home. At the pier, I would shake Flynn's hand, thank him for a lovely day, and go to my apartment. I could probably finish the postcard I started at work yesterday while I watched something on Food Network. I had gone to Alcatraz with

Flynn. That was enough rebounding for now.

Aleena would be annoyed. She would probably tell me I needed to see a therapist—a real one that would help me stop sabotaging myself and would teach me little tricks so I would stop overthinking everything. She would probably even make up a proverb for me, something ridiculous like "She who thinks too big lives too little." I rolled my eyes. Now I was making up my own proverbs.

But maybe my proverb was right. I can't even remember when I dated someone with no thoughts of the future. I was always looking for "the one," for true love, the grand romance that would last forever. Was I even capable of enjoying myself in the moment with no thought of what came later?

I didn't know. I always thought about the big picture, and not just in dating. In third grade I asked Mom for a cd of classical music, not so I could lose myself in the beauty of it, but because Mrs. Sharp had told us that classical music would help us perform better when we started taking algebra and calculus. Almost everything I've ever done has been with a purpose in mind, never just for fun. I've always thought things through and looked ahead, and when it comes to dating, look where all that thinking has got me.

Nowhere.

I had to be doing something wrong. Was this it? Was my love life a disaster because I overthought everything? Was I too worried and uptight? Was the universe trying to tell me to chill out?

I glanced at Flynn. My neurosis probably had him eager to end this little playdate. I wouldn't blame him. I had flat-out told him he didn't interest me. I had even said I was scared of him.

I looked down at the swirling, inky-blue water and made a resolution. I knew it would be harder than many New Year's resolutions I'd made during my life, but I was determined to try to see it through.

I would relax. I would go with the flow. I'd quit overthinking every little thing and try to enjoy myself. Like a ball that's been dropped off a building, I would roll wherever gravity decided to send me.

At least for today.

"You're frowning again." Flynn said when we reached the sidewalk.

I jumped like I had been caught. "I am? Sorry."

Flynn patted his stomach. "I'm hungry. Want to get something to eat?"

I had a quick thought about what this question meant for my future, but I quickly squashed it and pictured a ball rolling down a hill.

I smiled. "I'd love to."

Chapter 5

"Do you have a favorite place to eat around here?" Flynn asked.

"If we go left, there's Fog City Diner. If we go right, we can go to Boudin Bakery and Café."

"Which would you suggest for an out-of-towner?"

"That's hard. They're both so good. But probably Fog City. It's sort of a San Francisco institution."

"Then let's go there."

We walked down The Embarcadero toward the restaurant. I found our walking pace interesting.

In tenth grade, a self-defense specialist came to visit our health class. There had been three assaults in Fairfield, and Mrs. Stanfield, our teacher, wanted us to learn how to avoid being a victim. The man who came was big and spent most of the time trying to scare the socks off us with horror stories from his years on the police force in Modesto. I think he got a little thrill from most of the girls gasping. He showed us a few moves we could use if we were attacked, but I was pretty skeptical. When Paige Gentry, a tiny blonde with huge eyes, knocked the man over, I suspected he was adding a World Cup-worthy flop for emphasis. It made me suspicious of all his self-defense moves.

I did come away with one piece of advice that made sense and stuck with me. "Walk quickly and with a purpose. If you look like you know where you're going, people will be less likely to bother you."

I could do that. I had long legs, so my brisk pace was a smaller person's jog.

Flynn's legs were even longer than mine and with his athletic build, I would have thought he would move rapidly, but several times I found myself having to shorten my usual stride to keep pace with him. Flynn strolled. He ambled. He meandered. I smiled at the words that popped into my mind. I couldn't remember ever having used the word "meandered" before. But Flynn was meandering.

We stopped and watched a bright yellow sailboat skim through the water until it disappeared behind a building. Two seagulls fought over the remains of a sandwich that had missed a garbage can. Neither of them needed the food. They were both fat and greedy and I wanted to shoo them away and let some of the hungrier birds enjoy the feast.

What would have usually taken me five minutes to walk took more than twice that.

Fog City Diner is a San Francisco landmark. Located on a pointed piece of land where Battery and The Embarcadero meet, its curved wood and glass walls commanded attention.

We sat on a polished wood bench on the Battery Street side of the restaurant while we waited for them to call Flynn's name. Flynn sat slightly facing me, his arm resting casually on the back of the bench.

"Do you know where Geary Street is?" he asked.

"I think it's by Union Square somewhere." Flynn raised his eyebrows in a question. "You probably don't know where Union Square is, do you?"

Flynn shook his head. "No, but that sounds familiar. I think Bruce might have mentioned Union Square."

"Union Square is about a mile and a half that way." I pointed across the street. "What's not far from Union Square?"

"Geary Street."

I laughed at our talking in circles. "And what's on Geary Street?"

"Bruce's office."

"Ah. And he's an architect?"

"Right. When we were younger we thought we'd move to Glasgow. Bruce would be a famous architect and I would build the things he designed."

"You wanted to be a builder?"

"Aye. I am a builder. Sort of. I went to school in Edinburgh and I've got my construction license. Sadly, there's not much building to be done in Stornoway. But I did build a house."

"You built your house?"

"Naw. Not mine. Someday I might build me a house. I built a house for Jessie's brother and his wife."

"Maybe you should move to San Francisco and build Bruce's designs."

Flynn looked at me out of the corner of his eye. "Are ya already inviting me to stay?"

Sometimes I hate my face. Okay, not my face exactly, but all the little capillaries that betray me so often. I turned away, pretending to look down the street, when I was really just trying to hide my flushed cheeks.

"Only if you want to. To work with Bruce, I mean."

"I don't know if I'd even follow Bruce to Glasgow now. I can't leave Mum alone."

"She could move with you."

"Naw. She was born in Stornoway, and she says she'll die there. And she wouldn't want to leave the store. It meant too much to Dad."

"So you've given up building?"

"Given it up. Put it on hold. I guess I'm just waiting for a building boom on the Isle." Flynn laughed. He had a really good laugh. It was like his entire body wanted in on the fun. "If ya saw the Isle, you would know why that's funny. I don't think there will ever be a building boom there. At least I know how to use all the tools I sell. That comes in handy." I would have felt bad for Flynn and his unfulfilled dream, but he didn't seem sad. He seemed like a roll-with-the-punches kind of guy. Maybe I could learn something from him.

"Why did Bruce move to San Francisco?" I asked.

"A girl."

"Really?"

"Things didn't work out for 'em, but he liked America. Didn't make Mum too happy, though."

"What about you? Were you unhappy he stayed?"

Flynn shrugged. "I miss him. We were best friends."

I nodded. "I would hate it if my brother or sister moved halfway around the world."

"Yeah, but I'm glad he's happy."

"Macgruger?" A tall man with a goatee sculpted into intricate curlicues and points called Flynn's name from the open door. We followed him to a booth by the window.

"Now that looks like it'd be a bother to take care of," Flynn said, rubbing his chin, when the man was out of earshot.

I shook my head. "Way too much maintenance. That's much better," I said, pointing at his chin.

Flynn ran his hand over his own short whiskers and then opened his menu. "Have you always lived in San Franscisco?"

"Just since I graduated four years ago," I said. "I moved here when I got the job at Jayne Fife." I told Flynn about Fairfield while we looked over the menu.

"I can see why Bruce likes it here. There are so many people, and there's so much to do. Very different than The Isle of Lewis. There are less than twenty thousand people on the whole island. I think Bruce's apartment building has that many people."

"What kinds of things do you do on the Isle of Lewis?" I felt a little pretentious saying the name. What would it be like to live on an isle?

"I play rugby and I golf."

"My friend, Angus, golfs. He's made me try a few times, but I'm not any good."

"In Stornoway, you share the course with the sheep."

"Seriously? What if you hit one with a golf ball?"

"That's happened. But it's riskier for the golfers. You never know what your shoe or your ball is going to land in."

I laughed. "That's probably the sheep's way of sticking up for their friends who've been hit by golf balls."

"The sheep are winning. I've never hit one of them, but I've had to clean more than my share of shoes."

"I'll bet it's pretty there. Even the name—Isle of Lewis—sounds beautiful. Is it as pretty as it sounds?"

A waitress came and took our order.

"It's gorgeous. Some say it's the most beautiful place on earth. There are songs written about it. I'd sing one for ya, but I'm tryin' not to scare you away." Flynn winked.

"You sing that bad?"

"No. I've been told I have the voice of an angel." Flynn's teasing smile was way too cute.

"Then why would it scare me?"

"It might make me hard to resist."

"Oh brother." I rolled my eyes. "I'm not afraid of you." I looked directly at him, my expression serious.

"Maybe I should be afraid of *you*." Flynn laughed. "Isn't there a song about San Francisco?"

"'I Left My Heart in San Francisco,' and no, I'm not singing it for you."

"You're that bad, huh?"

"No one's told me I sound like an angel," I said.

"Sounds like a sad song."

"I guess it is." I thought for a moment. "I think I only know the line that says 'I left my heart in San Francisco.'"

"That is a sad song. The song about Stornoway is a happy one."

A few minutes later, the waitress brought our food—grilled lamb kabobs for Flynn and a salmon sandwich for me. It was a pleasant, comfortable lunch.

The breeze felt warm after the air conditioning in Fog City Diner. A woman jogged toward us pushing a stroller. When she got close enough for us to see inside it, we saw that it held a fluffy, white Bichon Frise.

Flynn turned toward me, a question on his face. He pointed at the stroller that was now crossing the street. "Did I really just see a dog in a pram?"

I laughed. "There's a woman on my street that jogs with her giant schnauzer in a stroller."

Flynn shook his head.

I wasn't sure what would happen next, but I was determined to "go with the flow." Maybe there was no flow going and I would be home working in half an hour. And then a strange thing happened. Flynn looked around and then pointed across the street.

"That way to Union Square?"

I nodded.

"Shall we?" he asked.

And that was that. I didn't know if we were actually headed to Union Square or if we were on our way to Bruce's office, but it didn't really matter. As long as Flynn was including me in his afternoon, I would stick around.

I've walked the streets of San Francisco for years, but I usually walk briskly from one place to another. It was a whole new experience to meander the streets with Flynn. We looked in windows. We paused to read a sign posted on a light pole about Tinkerbell, a lost Alaskan Husky.

"He's probably not really lost," Flynn said. "He probably ran away. He was tired of being called Tinkerbell."

Flynn looked at a man walking toward us. He elbowed me and whispered, "Do you think he's a rapper?" He nodded toward the man whose black jeans rode well below his hips. He wore a long, white parka, in spite of the heat, and a 49ers baseball cap that rested at a jaunty angle. Reflecting sunglasses made his eyes impossible to see. Several large, gold chains hung around his neck and the hand we could see was covered in gaudy rings. The other hand was under his coat, behind his back. He swaggered by, every part of his body fluid and rhythmic.

"I guess he might be."

"When I was a kid, I thought America was all rappers and cowboys, but that's the first rapper I've seen since I got here and I haven't seen a single cowboy."

"Rappers and cowboys?" I laughed. "Why did you think that?"

"MTV and American movies, I guess. Now I can say I've seen a rapper, but I'll be disappointed if I go home without seeing a single cowboy."

I looked up at Flynn's face to see if he was serious and caught him grinning at me.

"I guess you can count him as your rapper, even though he might be the worst rapper in the world."

"Did you see that swagger? Of course he can rap."

We started walking again. "I don't know. The way he moved makes me think he's probably a good dancer, but I don't know if he can rap."

"I'm calling him a rapper."

"If you feel good about that," I said.

Flynn grinned. "I do. Now I just need to see a cowboy."

"Maybe you'll have to rent a western."

"I've got five more days. I'm not giving up yet."

I thought we were headed toward Union Square, but we took the most roundabout way possible. I was seeing places I hadn't known existed. We shared a piece of carrot cake at a tiny bakery I had never heard of but knew I would be returning to. We talked and laughed and teased as we went.

"All Classics," I said, pointing to a record store across the street. "Shall we see if they have 'I Left My Heart in San Francisco?'"

Flynn took my hand and headed across the street. I looked around, hoping we weren't going to get cited for jaywalking or worse, hit by a car.

"And we can see if they have 'Lovely Stornoway.'"

I laughed. "Right. I'll buy you dinner if they have that one."

Flynn let go of my hand when we were on the sidewalk. "And I'll let you." He held the door open for me and then headed to the girl with Cindy Brady pigtails behind the counter.

I turned away, hoping I didn't look as flushed as I felt. Why was I talking about dinner? Going with the flow didn't mean me putting ideas in Flynn's head. I didn't want him to think I was hoping for anything. I wasn't even sure if I was hoping for the day to extend to dinner. And here I was, overthinking again.

I made my way to the section with a hanging sign that said "Classics." The store had four Tony Bennett CDs and I was excited to find that "I Left My Heart in San Francisco" was on two of them.

My phone vibrated in my pocket. It was a text from Aleena, asking if I'd had a good time. I quickly responded that I was still with him and immediately she texted back.

Aleena: yay! Things must be going well. Just remember, he's your rebound. Don't go falling in love and moving to Scotland or I'll be sorry I encouraged this.

No way was I giving her the satisfaction of responding to that. I glanced at the screen of my phone before I put it away and paused. Was it really almost five? We had been wandering together for almost four hours.

Flynn was leaning casually against the counter. "She's looking it up," he said.

"Yeah, um, it looks like we don't have it. In fact, I don't see anything at all by that guy."

"Calum Kennedy."

"Yeah. Him."

"Well thank you for looking."

I put the Tony Bennett CD on the counter. "I'll take this," I said to the clerk then turned to Flynn. "Looks like I did better than you."

"I was at a substantial disadvantage, I think."

"Excuses, excuses."

I paid the clerk. When we emerged onto the sidewalk, I handed the little paper bag to Flynn. "This is for you. A little souvenir to help you remember San Francisco."

"Thank you, Charlotte." He tucked the CD into his bag of books and then pulled me into a quick side hug. "But don't you fret. I don't think I'll be forgetting San Francisco any time soon." He squeezed my shoulder and left his hand there as we started to walk. When he moved his hand, I realized I probably wouldn't be forgetting Scotland any time soon, either. And I've never even been there.

Chapter 6

$\mathcal{I}$ found myself distracted and unproductive on Wednesday morning. Just after I had arrived, my twin brother, Will, had called to check on my mental and emotional state.

"How're you holding up, Chuck?"

"I'm okay. The first few days were rough, but now I'm back in the saddle." I did my best to sound like I was my normal, pre-heartbroken self.

"Back in the saddle?" Will sounded skeptical.

"Isn't that what you're supposed to do when you get bucked off a horse? Jump back on?"

"Well, didn't you technically get bucked off six months ago?"

"I used that time to brush myself off."

"So that's what you were doing? I guess we didn't need to worry about you after all?" Will has always looked out for me, but still, his serious tone took me by surprise.

"You were worried?"

"Of course. We all were."

"So you've all been talking about me behind my

back?" We both laughed.

When I was about thirteen, I had complained to Mom and Dad that Will and Angus were talking about me behind my back. We'd had a lengthy discussion about how it's not really talking behind your back if you only say things you would say in front of someone. To prove their point, they had called Will and Angus in and had me look at them while they repeated the conversation they'd just had. As it turned out, it was terribly embarrassing for all three of us.

While I stood there and watched, Angus told Will what some of the kids at school had said about me. "Mr. Harbaugh was teaching us about genetics and Jim and Alan leaned over and said, 'Too bad for Will's sister. She must have got all the giant genes. She's an Amazon. She's taller than any boy in our class."

"Did they get in trouble?" Will asked. He rolled his eyes at us, not enjoying this little re-creation.

"No. Mr. Harbaugh didn't hear them. But I told them they were just jealous and if she was a freak then every supermodel was a freak, too."

Angus's face had turned redder and redder as he told the story and I'm pretty sure mine had done the same.

"Thank you, Angus," my dad had said.

Mom had put her hand on my shoulder. "See, Charlotte. If it's something they can say to your face, then it's not a mean thing to talk behind your back. Sometimes we have to talk about each other because we care about each other." Then she had turned to the boys. "Just be sure you only say things you would be willing to say to Charlotte's face."

They had nodded and made a hasty escape to the back yard.

"You haven't bounced back the way you usually do, Chuck," Will said. "It seems like you took the breakup with Kyle especially hard."

"Yeah, I did. But I'm bouncing back now, so you can tell everyone I'm A-okay."

A few minutes after we hung up, Mom called. "Will says you sound great and you're getting back on the horse."

I laughed. "That didn't take long."

"He knows I've been worried about you. He probably just wanted to put my mind at ease."

"You don't need to worry, Mom. I'm okay."

"What's this about the saddle and the horse?"

"I went on a date yesterday."

"That's great, honey. Did you have a nice time?"

"Yeah. It was better than I expected."

"How do you know him?"

"I met him at Imperial Palace when Aleena and I went there for lunch last week. He's from Scotland. He's in the states visiting his brother."

"Scotland?"

"The Isle of Lewis, to be exact." Mom took a deep breath. "What's wrong, Mom?"

"Nothing's wrong. I guess I would have been happier to hear this if your date was from somewhere a little closer to home."

"You don't need to worry. It wasn't even really a date date. I'm just testing the waters again, you know?"

"I'd rather you tested the waters here in the bay area."

We laughed. "The bay area waters have been awesome for me, haven't they?"

"Oh, Charlotte."

"It's okay, Mom. You don't need to worry. I'm not moving to Scotland."

I nearly gave up on work when Aleena called a short time later. She wanted a complete report on yesterday's activities and to tell me that Angus had called and they were going to dinner on Friday.

I had been at my desk nearly two hours and the only work I had accomplished was emailing Huck at Adventureland (yes, that is really his name) to let him know I would be sending him proofs by the end of the day.

I pulled out my pencils and markers and started coloring the last postcard, marveling at the good fortune that gave me a job that paid me to color. I was shading a red bumper car when my cell phone chirped. I was surprised to see Flynn's number.

"Hello."

"Charlotte." The sound of Flynn saying my name sounded so exotic and lovely. I needed to record him saying it over and over so I could listen to it when I needed a little pick-me-up. I was replaying the lilt of his pronunciation in my mind when he said it again, but this time as a question. "Charlotte?" That had worked out nicely.

"Yes. Hi Flynn. How's it going?"

"Good. I'm swimming here at Bruce's pool while both you and Bruce are working. It feels wrong, somehow."

"Well, you are on vacation so you shouldn't feel

guilty."

"A vacation by myself, unfortunately, which isn't nearly as fun as vacationing with someone else. By the way, thank you for taking the day off yesterday. I had a grand time."

"I did too. Thanks for inviting me. Where did you and Bruce end up going to dinner?"

"We went to a place called Marcroft. Have you been there?"

"I don't think so."

"It was good. You should try it sometime."

"I will. I'm sorry Bruce has been so busy while you're here," I said.

"Aye, so is he. But they moved up the deadline on his biggest project ever. He doesn't have to work Saturday or Sunday so we'll do something fun."

"Aren't you leaving Sunday?"

"Aye, but not until late. We'll have all day."

"That's good."

"So, Charlotte."

"Yes?"

"Speaking of Bruce, he suggested I see if you can help me out again."

"Help you with what?" I have to admit the idea that I might see him again made me more excited than I had expected.

"If ya can't pull it off, no worries, but I want to see more of the Pacific Ocean. Bruce said I should go to Big Sur and a town called Carmel."

I smiled when he pronounced it like the candy.

"I guess it's a few hours away, so I'd like to make it a

day trip. Any chance I could schedule an appointment with ya for the day?"

I almost laughed at his avoidance of the word "date." I mentally checked off the projects I was working on and knew I was on track with all of them. I had plenty of vacation days and Jayne would probably sing and dance if she knew I was seeing Flynn again.

"I'll have to clear it with my boss, but I think I can."

"Brilliant." Flynn's delight made me even more excited. I wasn't sure if his enthusiasm was because he wanted to see me again or because he wouldn't have to go sightseeing alone. It really didn't matter. Except I guess it did a little. It occurred to me that I hoped he actually wanted to see me again and I wasn't just a choice born of desperation.

"I'm going to rent a car. Bruce is going to the project site tomorrow, so I can't take his."

"Don't waste your money renting a car. I can drive." Then I remembered the size of my car. "Unless a Volkswagen Bug would be too uncomfortable. You're a big guy."

Flynn laughed. "My car at home is an MG. Not much bigger than a Bug. I don't want to trouble ya though. I can rent a car."

"If you don't mind the size, you should save your money. We can take my car."

It didn't take long to iron out the details for the next morning. When I got off the phone, I walked to Jayne's office. The door was open so I knocked on the door frame.

"Charlotte. Come in. Sit down."

I sat down opposite her. Was it really less than a week

since she had told me about Kyle? Time was such a strange thing

"How are you doing?" Jayne gave me a sympathetic smile.

"I'm okay. I'm trying not to think about Kyle and it's helping. When I do think about it, I know he and Wyatt make a good team, so I feel a little less awful." Jayne nodded. "The reason I'm here is because I wanted to see about taking another day off tomorrow."

Jayne's expression changed from pity to party so fast I couldn't help but laugh. "Is this because of your handsome highlander?"

I rolled my eyes. "Really? Handsome highlander? And he's not mine."

"Whatever. Is this about *him*?"

"Yes. His brother is still tied up with work."

"So he says." She waggled her eyebrows at me.

"He is. He's working on a big project and they moved the date up."

Jayne flicked her hand at me. "Fine. Seems pretty convenient, but I'll go with it."

"Anyway." I dragged out the word for effect. "He wants to go to Carmel and Big Sur and invited me along. Is there any reason I can't go?"

"You've got Adventureland about finished, right?"

"Sending the proofs out this afternoon."

"What else are you working on?"

"I've got the lunch boxes for Six Flags and the package for Trees of Mystery and the playing cards for Jackpot. I'm ahead of schedule on all of those."

"Of course you are. Go have fun tomorrow."

"Thanks, Jayne."

I was almost out the door when she stopped me.

"Charlotte. I'm glad you're having fun with this guy, but don't fall for him. I can't have you moving to Scotland."

I shook my head. "Why does everyone keep saying that?"

"Because contrary to what you might think, one of these days the odds are going to be in your favor, and you're going to fall madly in love with someone who's smart enough not to let you get away."

What a sap I am. Suddenly I was overcome with emotion. I put my hand on my chin to keep it still and swallowed hard. When I could speak without my voice cracking, I said, "Thank you, Jayne."

She nodded twice and I left.

"I should have let you rent a car," I said as Flynn origamied himself into the passenger seat of my bug. He adjusted the seat back as far as it would go, which was about an inch farther than it had been when he squeezed in.

"No, this is fine. Really. I wanted to ask if you'd care if I drove back though. I'd like to say I drove the California coast."

"Of course. Do you want to drive now?"

"Naw. The way back is good. I'll just enjoy the view as we go." He looked at me pointedly, his eyes playful. I tried to ignore my warm cheeks and I turned to check out the back window, which was a mistake because my car is so small it put our faces much too close together. If my cheeks were warm before, they were burning now. "Don't fret. I'm talking about the view of the ocean, although you look very pretty this morning."

I wasn't sure what to say. Thank you? You look really nice too? Don't forget this isn't a real date? I spent so long wondering what I should say that it became awkward to say anything, so instead, I put the car in reverse and backed out of the parking place.

I felt bad for Flynn stuffed into the car like a Jack-in-the-Box. It was just too small for him. Angus had often been squeezed in here like this, but that was Angus, and it was usually just for a few minutes. This would be for a whole day. I regretted my offer and wished we were in a comfortable sedan.

"What's chewin' on ya today?"

"What?"

"You're wearing that frown again so I know you're thinking on something."

"I do that a lot lately, don't I?"

"So it's me brings it outa ya?"

I shook my head. "I didn't realize I looked upset when I was thinking. Sorry. I was just thinking about how uncomfortable you're going to be spending so long in my little car." I smiled to show him I wasn't angry.

Flynn patted my hand on the steering wheel. "I really will be fine. My car's not much bigger than this and I've survived this long. We'll just have to pull over and see the sights along the way and stretch our legs." His hand completely covered mine. I have long fingers, so that's a rare thing. I thought about Kyle's hands. They were about the same size as mine. Had I ever dated anyone with hands as large as Flynn's? I couldn't think of anyone.

I could feel Flynn looking at me. I didn't want to appear angry or deep in thought so I said the first thing I thought of. "You have really large hands." Oh brother. Like he didn't know that.

Flynn held his hands out in front of him and I noticed they were covered in the same freckles as his face.

"I could have played basketball if I'd grown up here, but there's not a lot of basketball in Stornoway."

"I don't think I've ever dated anyone with such long fingers." I groaned inside because I could tell by Flynn's mischievous look that I had said the wrong thing.

"So you're calling this a date?"

I shook my head and shrugged and Flynn laughed.

"Good."

I wasn't sure what to say to that and Flynn must have been at a loss, as well, because neither of us spoke for several minutes. It wasn't an uncomfortable silence. It felt friendly and easy. I made my way through the morning traffic and merged onto the freeway that would take us to the Pacific Coast Highway.

"Have you dated a lot of men with stubby fingers?"

I snort laughed and Flynn joined me. On the laughing part.

"Sorry. I hate that I snort sometimes."

"It doesn't bother me."

"You caught me off guard."

"My question?"

I nodded, still laughing.

"I was just curious. You mentioned that mine were the largest hands you've dated. I wondered if you've dated a lot."

I sighed.

"Not a happy subject?" he asked.

"It's not that."

"You're still sad about the man you broke up with?"

I should have felt uncomfortable talking about guys and dating with a man I was sort of dating for only the second time, but I didn't. There was something strangely easy about talking to Flynn. Maybe it was the fact that he lived on the other side of the world that seemed to give me the freedom to say what I was thinking instead of filtering myself. Or maybe it was just that he was warm and friendly and had a quick, good-natured smile.

"Yeah. I'm still sad about that. He's engaged now." Flynn waited, like he expected me to say more. "But it's not just him. I sort of have a dating reputation that isn't easy to live with."

"You have a reputation?"

I laughed. "That didn't come out right. Does a girl having a 'reputation' mean the same in Scotland that it does here?" I put air quotes around "reputation."

"Probably. But you don't seem like a girl with that kind of reputation, so you must mean something else."

I nodded. "I do." And then I told Flynn about being called the husband maker. I didn't go into specifics about every guy, but enough that he understood I wasn't joking and that it was a well-earned nickname. He asked a few questions, but mostly he listened without laughing at me.

When I finished talking, he looked thoughtful for a few minutes. I started to think he had nothing to say about the sad tale I had just shared, but finally he spoke.

"You're lookin' at it as a bad thing, but I think that's wrong."

"There's a good way to look at it?" I glanced at him skeptically.

"Ya make men think about growin' up and settlin' down. So they do."

"With someone else." I was glad I needed to watch the road. I didn't want to look at him looking at me.

"I guess they weren't the right one for you. But Charlotte—" why did I melt when he said my name?—"ya make them think gettin' married would be a good thing. It might not be great for you, but I think you should take it as a compliment."

I didn't speak. For the second time in two days, someone had chiseled away at the shell that had been forming over my once hopeful heart. I blinked hard. It was one thing to feel comfortable enough with Flynn to tell him about my nickname. It was quite another to melt into a weepy mess when we hardly knew each other. But his words did something to me. They made me a little teary, but that wasn't all. They softened some of that shell. For more than six months, fear had been calcifying there, making my hope harder and harder to find. Would every man find happiness with someone else? Would there ever be a man who found his happiness in me?

"Thanks, Flynn," I finally said. I had never been so open about dating and my worries with a man before. I had always been afraid it made me look lacking in some way. But Flynn was easy to talk to. I wondered if it was because this was a short-term arrangement or if it was just Flynn. Whatever it was, the openness was nice.

"Maybe I should be the one who's scared, aye?" His voice was teasing again.

"You sure you want to call this a date?" I asked. "Are you ready to go home and get married?"

"Ah, Charlotte. You don't scare me at all."

Chapter 7

The Interstate took us west and it wasn't long before eight lanes of traffic narrowed to four and eventually two. We turned south on the Pacific Coast Highway. I knew the ocean was to our right, but a thick fog hugged the coastline, blocking our view of the water. As we drove, the sun rose higher and the cottony billows melted to a haze and then burnt away completely to reveal the steep cliffs and the choppy water beyond.

"I didn't know California and Scotland had so much in common," Flynn said. "Don't much think of fog when you think of California."

"The bay area gets lots of fog but it usually burns off in the morning."

"The sun must not burn as hot in Scotland because sometimes the fog lasts all day. And Scotland is greener, I think," Flynn said. The steep hills rising to our left were covered with brush and a pale carpet of springtime grass.

"This is actually pretty green for right here. In the summer this will be mostly brown. But it gets greener the farther south we go, down around the golf courses and south of Carmel."

"I said Carmel wrong yesterday, didn't I?"

I laughed. "You said it like the candy."

"You were kind not to make fun of me."

"It's an easy mistake to make. I'm sure if I came to Scotland, I would mispronounce plenty of things."

"Are you going to come visit my fair country?"

"I said *if* I came to Scotland."

"I think that's a grand idea. You'd like Scotland, and if ya came to Stornoway, ya might never want to leave. They say a piece of heaven broke off and landed in the cold North Sea and when people discovered it, they called it the Isle of Lewis."

"You sound like a tour guide."

"If ya came ta Lewis I'd be your guide. Pay ya back for showing me around."

"Speaking of guide, is there anything in particular you want to see on this little day trip?" I had spent the evening googling sites to see and had a few ideas of places to go, but if Flynn had something in mind, I didn't want to leave it out.

"Wherever you want to take me. I'm at your mercy."

Something about him putting his entire day in my hands made me nervous and excited. I wanted to make this day a day he'd remember long after he went back to Scotland.

My little, old car roared down the highway. The radio worked but music sounded tinny, and there was a constant background buzz, so I rarely turned it on, and Flynn didn't ask me to. Conversation was surprisingly effortless. We fell into a comfortable rhythm of lively talking and then quiet, almost like the rattling hum of the engine had temporarily hypnotized us. Neither of us felt the need to fill the quiet moments, and we didn't talk unless we had something to say.

"Does this road continue north into Oregon?"

"No. It starts north of San Francisco and ends before it hits Mexico. It runs along about three fourths of the California coast. The section we're driving today, that goes to Big Sur, was the first section of the road that was finished. That was in the 1930s. Other pieces were done at different times. They weren't completely linked together until 1964."

I could feel Flynn watching me, and I glanced over to see his wide smile.

"What's so funny?"

"Did you study the history of this road in school?"

I laughed. "No. I studied it last night. On the internet. So I could tell you about it."

"Is that true?"

I shrugged. "It's no big deal. I just wanted to be sure I could tell you about some of the things we see."

"That was nice of you."

"Not really. If I'm going to be your tour guide, I should do it right. Besides, I just want you to enjoy your visit. Especially since Bruce has been so tied up. It'd be awful to spend money on a big trip like this and not get to see very much."

"You're a thoughtful lass, Charlotte."

"Look at the rocks out there." I wanted to distract him from my flushed face, so I pointed at the large rocks that rose out of the ocean. Waves crashed against them, sending up a wild spray.

"Your ocean looks friendlier than mine. The waters around Stornoway are gray and mysterious."

It wasn't quite lunchtime when the terrain began to flatten out and civilization reappeared. "You want to see the golf courses first?"

"I love golf."

"Do all Scots love it?"

"No. It's a hard sport. Some hate it. My dad broke so many golf clubs, my mum told him he couldn't golf anymore."

"Seriously?"

"She told him we couldn't afford to keep replacing clubs, so if he didn't control his temper, he'd have to quit golf."

"So did he quit?"

"Naw. He told her he was going to start selling clubs at the store, so he dedicated one corner of the store to golf equipment. He'd just order extras so when he would ruin one, he'd just subtract another one from the inventory. She thought he'd quit losing his temper, because he always came home with his clubs in good shape. We never told her to check the rubbish bin behind the store."

We laughed.

"Are you an angry golfer?"

"Naw, but Bruce has been known to throw a club or two."

I pulled into a turnout and reached for a file folder in the back seat.

"Are you a good navigator?" I asked.

"Hawl?" It took me a second, but then I remembered

that "hawl" means excuse me.

"Following a map?"

"Oh, ya. I can do that."

I pulled out a paper that I had printed off the night before with a map of the roads that lead through the golf courses. "There are a few places we can pull over and see things. They're marked. Just let me know which ones you want to see."

For more than an hour we toured golf courses. We didn't walk the courses but some had lookouts or views from the club house. Flynn's favorite was Pebble Beach. Mine was Spyglass Hill. It had so many flowers.

"Would you take our picture with it?" Flynn asked an older man standing on the boardwalk with us. We were looking out at the Lone Cypress, a landmark at Pebble Beach.

"Be happy to," the man said and took Flynn's camera.

We stood together and smiled. The man held Flynn's camera under his arm, carefully removed his glasses, and put them in his pocket. Then he aimed the camera in our direction.

"Move in a little closer so I can get a better view of the tree." The man winked at us. Flynn pulled me close to his side and the man snapped a picture. "Now just hold tight a minute. Let me see if this is a good one."

Flynn and I stood there for a few moments while the man held the camera at arm's length and studied the picture. "I think I'll take another one. You look too serious. Smile kids." We smiled, and the man snapped a couple more pictures. When we started to move apart, he grunted and gave us a stern look. We didn't move.

It took him a moment, but then he found the button and looked through the pictures. "You know, kids, when I was your age, we used film." He held the camera farther away from him and tilted his head. "You probably don't even know what film is."

I stifled a giggle. "Does he think we're ten?" I said quietly and Flynn squeezed my shoulder.

"Aye. I remember it," Flynn said to the man.

"I hope you appreciate these new-fangled cameras." He waved Flynn's camera in the air. "You can take as many pictures as you want until you get a good one. I remember shooting entire rolls of film and until we had it developed, we didn't know if a single picture had turned out or not. And did you know we even had to pay for the ones that didn't turn out?"

"That's madness," Flynn said.

"Hold still." The man held up the camera again and snapped another picture.

"I remember taking a whole roll of film and I'll be darned if not one picture turned out. Half of them were blurry and the rest were black. I spent $3.00 on the film and $4.00 to have it developed and not one picture turned out."

He snapped two more pictures. "Are you not smiling?" Flynn whispered, glancing at me.

"I'm smiling," I said through my teeth. Flynn was snickering.

"Stop it." I elbowed him.

"Let's try another one. Don't make him do all the work, young lady. Put your arm around him and look like you like each other. You don't want people thinking you were fighting on your honeymoon."

I stifled a snort.

"This is your honeymoon, right?"

"Aye, but it is," Flynn said. "How could ya tell?"

"I've always had an eye for newlyweds. Even when they're fighting. Phyllis used to say it was a gift. She was my wife. She had hair the same color as yours, young lady."

"Get over here, little hen," Flynn said, pulling me in front of him. He wrapped his arms around my stomach and snuggled forward until his cheek rested on mine. His arms were warm, the stubble on his face, scratchy and soft at the same time. It felt wonderful and I resisted the urge to rub my cheek against his.

"That's better. Let me take a couple of these and you can choose the best one," he said.

"Little hen?" I whispered.

"Shhh."

The old man held the camera away and looked at the picture he had just taken. "Ah, that's a nice one." I felt disappointed when Flynn stepped away to retrieve his camera.

"Be glad you don't have to get these developed. My brother owned a little hut and you could drive up and drop off your film, just like McDonalds. We thought it was fast to be able to see our pictures in an hour. Here you kids can look at all these pictures in just seconds."

"Thank ya," Flynn said, his accent strong.

"I'm sure you kids have quite a story about how you met, but I won't keep you from your honeymoon. Congratulations. Be happy together."

"Thanks," I said.

"Ah, but we sure will," Flynn said.

We held it together until the old man was gone and then we both collapsed onto a bench laughing.

"Little hen? What is that?"

"It's an endearment. It's what we call our sweetheart."

"You call your sweetheart a hen? Doesn't sound very complimentary."

"Ah, but it is, my little hen." Flynn squeezed my shoulder. "Now let's enjoy the rest of our honeymoon."

I shook my head. "You let him think we were really newlyweds."

"I didn't want to spoil his record. He got some pretty good shots. Look at these."

I leaned closer and Flynn put his hand above the screen to block out the sun. Our arms brushed together as we scrolled through the pictures.

"This one's the best," Flynn said, stopping at the picture of me in his arms. "The tree looks nice and you look like you're about to burst."

"I held it together pretty good."

"Aye, we both did." Flynn put the camera around his neck. "What did he mean about getting your pictures from a hut?"

"I'm not sure what he was talking about."

As we walked back to my car, I suppressed the urge to reach for Flynn's hand. That was silliness. No matter how much I enjoyed his company, this would probably be the last day I ever saw him. Even though I was trying not to overthink the situation, I couldn't help but realize that holding his hand, or any other affectionate behavior, would just make me miss him when he went home. I didn't need anyone else to miss.

We were hungry by the time we arrived in Carmel. I parked the car on a little side road, close to a touristy street lined with restaurants and gift shops.

"Some of these remind me of home," Flynn said as we walked by little cottages that had been there for years.

We ate turkey and cranberry sandwiches at a little café that had outdoor seating. Flynn finished eating before I did. He folded his napkin, stretched out his legs to the side of the table, and rested his arms across his stomach.

"No need ta rush." He put his hand up when he saw me take two quick bites.

"I'm kind of a slow eater."

"We're not in a hurry." I slowed down, glad I could enjoy the last few bites of my sandwich. "Do ya come here often?"

"Not enough," I said between bites. "I should come more. It's nice to get out of the city sometimes."

Flynn grinned. "You come here ta get out of the city. Stornoway's the biggest town on the island and everyone there would think this *was* the city."

"I guess it's all a matter of perspective."

"Aye." I realized Flynn was watching me and I suddenly felt self-conscious.

"What?" I wiped my mouth with the napkin.

"Just thinkin'."

"About what?" I took a drink of water, not sure if I liked him looking at me like that.

"I'm just wonderin' who I'm going to marry now that I've dated the husband maker."

"I shouldn't have told you about that."

"Sure you should have. It's a talent."

I laughed and decided to play along. "Do you have a girlfriend at home?"

"Naw. I have some friends who are girls, but not a girlfriend."

"Well, you'll either hit it off with someone new, or you'll start to see one of those friends that are girls—" I used air quotes—"in a whole new way. You'll have to send me an announcement."

"Not an announcement. I'll send ya an invitation."

"I could make a vacation of it."

"But first I have to find a wife."

"Don't worry. You will."

"Will ya hate me if I break your little curse?"

"No. I think that would make me love you."

"Hmm. Now this is getting interesting."

I shook my head. "We should go." I scooted back my chair and stood. Flynn laughed at my abrupt ending to the conversation.

"Where to next?" he asked.

"Wherever you want."

"Maybe this would be a good place to pick up a gift for my mum."

We browsed our way down the street for a few blocks, looking in gift shops. Flynn bought a book called *California Maritime Archeology* for himself in one store, but we had made it almost back to the car and he still hadn't found a gift for his mom.

We stopped at a thatch-roofed bakery. It sat back from the street and had an English rose garden and a white, gated fence in front of it. The aroma of freshly baked cookies drew us in and we weren't disappointed. A young girl was emptying a baking sheet of warm, chocolate chip cookies directly to a plate in the display case.

While Flynn ordered two cookies, I wandered to a hutch in the corner. It was covered with crafts and jewelry. A silver chain with a small seahorse made of blue blown glass caught my eye.

Flynn wandered over holding a small paper bag with our cookies. "What did ya find?"

"This is pretty. Would your mom like something like this?" I asked, holding it up.

"Aye. That's nice." Flynn handed me the bag of cookies and held the pendant up to the light from the front window. "I'm just not sure. She doesn't wear a lot of jewelry." He hung the necklace back on the peg and held up a soft, fuzzy, knitted hat. It was bright red. "She'd like this, but it might be a little bright."

I took a bite of one of the cookies. "Mmm. This is good."

"Maybe I'll wait."

We finished our cookies as we looked in a few more gift shops and then walked to the car.

"Do ya think you can pick me up at the sweet shop? I think I'll get that cap for mum."

"You should get us another cookie while you're at it."

Flynn thumped the roof of the car. "I like your thinking."

I dropped him off in front of the little cottage and drove around the block a couple of times.

"She'll like this," he said, when he was back in the car. "It'll be easy to spot her when she takes her walks down by the water."

I reached over and felt the soft yarn ball on the hat. "It's so fluffy. I'm sure she'll love it."

Chapter 8

I hadn't been to Big Sur for more than two years, but little had changed. That was the beauty of it. You could always count on lovely hiking trails, beautiful beaches, and crashing waves.

We stopped just before Bixby Bridge and took more pictures before we continued down the coast to Pfeiffer Park. I had found a highly recommended hike on the internet that didn't disappoint. In under a mile, we moved from brush to tall trees, and finally to the beach. We removed our shoes and rolled up our pants as we walked in the sand.

"Somewhere out there is a place where the water comes through a rock tunnel," I said, repeating what I had learned the night before. "I'm not sure where it is."

The large, volcanic rocks out in the water were more like small islands.

"Let's see if we can find it," Flynn said.

We walked up and down the beach looking for the hole in the rock where the waves surged through in a spray. "I watched it on YouTube last night, so I know it's here somewhere."

The sand was hot, so we spent most of our time walking through the cold water. Some of the waves lapped gently around our feet, but a few of them hurtled into our legs, soaking the bottoms of our pants.

"Maybe I'll have to see it on YouTube," Flynn said after more than an hour and several trips up and down the beach, studying the rocks from all different angles.

I laughed. "Some tour guide I am. I guess I'll have to email you the link. It was pretty cool."

"Ah well, the water feels great and I had fun, so don't fret."

At other stops we saw the Point Sur Lighthouse and McWay Falls, an eighty foot waterfall that empties onto the sand before running into the ocean.

"Well, Charlotte," Flynn said as we began the drive north. "I think you're a brilliant guide. Today was perfect."

I smiled. "Except for the hole in the rock. It was fun showing you around. Oh, did you want to drive?"

"Is that okay?"

"I don't mind."

"Let's eat and then I'll drive from there."

Flynn leaned his seat back a little and rested his hand on the back of my seat. He looked comfortable and at ease, but the proximity of his hand made it impossible for me to relax. I was driving, so total relaxation was out of the question anyway, but just knowing his hand was so close put my nerves on end. If I leaned back at all, would I touch it? If I did, would he move it away or touch me back? We'd had such a good time together that part of me wanted more. But that would just make it sad for him to leave.

Who was I kidding? I liked Flynn. He was kind and funny and interesting. If he lived here, I would be hoping to see more of him and I would definitely be wanting to lean back into his hand and hope it was the start of something. But he didn't live here and he was leaving in three days.

I was overthinking again. There are plenty of people who would tell me to lighten up. They would say, "He's leaving. Have a wild, passionate fling and then say goodbye. No big deal."

But those other people aren't me and no matter how much fun we had together, I couldn't separate my heart from my actions, and my heart was too fragile right now to throw caution to the wind. It was because I wanted to lean back and touch his hand that I couldn't. Or wouldn't.

And then he brushed a few loose strands of my hair back and rested his hand lightly on the back of my neck, just under my ponytail, and I forgot all my rational thoughts.

"Are you okay?" Flynn asked.

I didn't dare move my head to look at him. It might cause his hand to move and now that it had touched me, I wanted it to stay there permanently.

"I'm good," I said looking at the road ahead of us.

"I can always tell when you're stewin' on a problem."

"You can?"

"Your face. It gives you away."

"I'm not stewin' at all."

"What are ya thinking about?"

No way was I going to say what I had been thinking.

Especially not with his hand resting gently against my skin. I had been thinking I didn't want it there, but that was craziness. That was like a man in the desert trying to convince himself that he didn't want any water because he was afraid he was seeing a mirage and he didn't want to be disappointed.

"You don't want to tell me?" Flynn asked.

"I'll tell you. I was thinking about mirages in the desert."

"And that had you unhappy?"

"Well, mirages are kind of unhappy things, right? You're dying of thirst and you see water up ahead and then you get closer and, too bad, it wasn't really water after all."

Flynn laughed. "Are you thirsty?" His thumb moved just behind my ear.

I smiled. "Maybe a little. Good thing we're almost back to Carmel."

"Here's something for you to think about," Flynn said when we were almost finished with dinner. He reclined, his arm on the back of the booth. "It's not life or death like a man dying in the desert, but I'd still like to know what you think."

I put down my fork and smiled. "You know how much I like to think about things."

"What if I want to see you again?"

It was difficult, but I think I managed to keep my breathing regular.

"Well, that's tricky since you live 4,851 miles from me."

The laughter in Flynn's eyes told me I shouldn't have been so specific.

"How do you know that?"

I'm pretty sure my face was the same color as the red, vinyl booth. I shrugged. "Google. You can find out pretty much anything you want to know on Google."

"And you wanted to know how far away I live?" I picked up the salt shaker and sprinkled salt onto my empty plate. "Does that mean you were planning to come visit me?"

"It means I was curious."

"Curious is a fine start."

I looked at his face to see if he was making fun of me. He wasn't. His eyes were sweet and smiling and it was hard to look away.

"I wasn't askin' ya to come to Scotland. I was just askin' for one more playdate."

"Isn't Bruce about finished with his project?"

"He won't be finished until after I'm gone, but I'm goin' to visit the site with him tomorrow morning, and he's taking the weekend off."

It wasn't what I wanted to say, but I knew I needed to say it. "You really should spend as much time with him as you can. He'd be sad if you came all this way and chose to spend your time with some girl instead of him."

Flynn leaned across the table and the corner of his mouth quirked up. "You're not just some girl, Charlotte."

Suddenly my stomach felt inhabited by an entire dance company raucously performing a jig. Probably a

Scottish jig.

"So will ya do something with me Friday night?"

"Flynn . . ."

"Bruce told me about the food trucks down by the pier. I can't remember what it's called."

"Off the Grid?"

"Aye, that's it. Bruce'll probably work late, so let's have dinner together Friday and then I'll spend the rest of my time here with him. Just a few hours. So I don't have ta go alone." Flynn reached across the table and put his hand on mine, stopping me from adding more salt to the little pile I had created.

I sighed. "Okay, but just to keep you company. Just so you're not a sad, pathetic tourist eating by yourself."

Flynn moved his hand and leaned back again. "Thanks, Charlotte. I'm not too good to accept your charity."

It was almost seven when we left the restaurant. I handed the keys to Flynn on the way to the car. "Your turn."

Flynn adjusted the driver's seat, which didn't help much since I'm tall and had it almost all the way back anyway.

When Flynn turned the key in the ignition, the engine turned over sluggishly but didn't start. "Is there a trick?"

"No. Sometimes it's just slow."

He tried again, but this time, it was even more lethargic. The third time he tried, the engine didn't even turn over. He turned the key a few more times, but nothing happened.

"I think we've got a dead battery."

"I've got jumper cables."

I retrieved the cables from the trunk while Flynn asked a couple that had just arrived if they could jumpstart the car. With the cables attached, the engine turned over slowly and then started.

We thanked the couple and pulled out of the parking spot. At a stop sign, the engine idled slowly and sounded like it might die, so Flynn pumped the gas to keep it going. A couple of blocks later, I saw an auto garage that looked open.

"Let's pull in there and see if they can tell us what's wrong. I don't want to be stuck on the road in the middle of nowhere."

"You barely caught me," a man in navy blue coveralls said, wiping his hands onto an oily rag. "We close at seven." He inclined his head toward a clock on the wall that showed we'd made it by only a few minutes.

"Thank you for looking. I don't want to be stranded between here and San Francisco."

"You wait in here and I'll take a quick look."

He left the room and we sat down in the cracked, vinyl chairs.

"See if I ever let you drive again," I said and we laughed.

"It's probably the battery or the alternator," Flynn said. "Let's hope it's the battery. That would be an easier fix."

We watched news headlines scroll past on the muted television until the mechanic returned a few minutes later.

"Ma'am, I'm afraid your alternator has gone out."

I tried not to laugh as I looked at Flynn. He grinned and shrugged.

"What do I need to do?"

"I'll have to order a part in, but I can probably have it ready to roll by tomorrow, late afternoon."

Now I wasn't laughing. Flynn came to the counter and stood by me.

"My aunt owns a nice bed and breakfast here in town. I can check with her and see if she's got any vacancies."

"That's okay. We'll figure something out."

"Sounds good. I'll call you if I run into any problems. Otherwise, you can come by and pick 'er up sometime after four."

We gathered a few things out of the car and then stepped out into the warm, evening air. The mechanic closed and locked the door as soon as we walked out. I let out a deep breath. My knees bumped my purse as I rocked back and forth, holding it with both hands in front of me. I looked to the right and then the left. I had no idea what to do.

"I'll do whatever you want, Charlotte. If you want to find a place to stay tonight, we can do that. If you want to find a way home, we'll find a way." I looked up at him. This might have been the most serious I had ever seen Flynn. "I feel terrible that I broke your car."

"You didn't do this. You just happened to be the one behind the wheel."

"Yaw, so much for driving."

I laughed and suddenly I felt better. "I couldn't have timed that better."

"Oh, ya knew it was about to go and ya put me behind the wheel?" Flynn laughed with me.

I shrugged. "Let's go find someplace to figure this out."

We walked about three blocks before we found a park. By the time we sat down at a picnic table, I had a few ideas.

"I'm going to see if I can get us a ride home and then I'll have someone drive me down Saturday."

"I could maybe come with ya tomorrow."

"No, you go with Bruce and see his project." No way was I going to interfere with the little bit of time they had left to spend together.

"Do you want us to bring you down Saturday?"

"No. I'll figure that out. You're on vacation and it's almost over." I was already punching some numbers into my phone. "I'm sending out a group text to see if any of my family can come down and pick us up tonight."

"And I'll call and see if Bruce is through for the day. Maybe he can come down."

It took only a couple of minutes to find out that Bruce wouldn't be finished until about nine. If we didn't find anyone else to come get us, he would then.

My phone vibrated.

Will: I can come in about an hour. What are you doing in Carmel?

I hadn't even written a response when it vibrated again.

Angus: Don't worry about it, Will. I'm on my way.

Me: Thanks Will. I took a friend sightseeing. Angus, are you sure you have time?

Angus: I just finished three days on so I'm off until Saturday evening. Where should I come?

Will: A friend, huh? Does this friend happen to be a man and is he by chance from another country?

Me: We're at a park in Carmel. It's on Juniper.

Dad: Thanks, Angus. Charlie, when was the last time you had your car serviced?

Me: It's been awhile, Dad. Will, I'm not sure I like your tone.

Dad: You shouldn't ever take a car on a long trip without it being serviced.

Me: You're right, Dad. I didn't really think about Big Sur being a long trip, but I guess the alternator showed me.

Will: You like my tone just fine. How is your Scottish "friend?"

Dad: I'm glad you're safe. Drive carefully, Angus. We owe you.

Angus: It's no problem.

Me: You're the best, Angus. Will, you're just a brat.

"Help is on the way," I said. "You can tell Bruce not to worry about it. Angus is coming."

"Your brother?"

"Practically. Our best friend."

"Lucky for us there's an ice cream shop right there." Flynn pointed at a little place just down the street. "And it looks like we've got a brilliant view of the sunset right here."

It was true. From our picnic table, there was a break in the buildings across the street and we would have a lovely view of the sky as the sun went down.

"Ice cream sounds heavenly," I said.

A short time later, we were sitting side by side on the picnic table, our feet on the bench, eating ice cream and watching the sky.

The sun felt bigger and golder than usual as it started its descent. Clouds on the horizon turned gold as the giant sun slipped lower. When it hit the sliver of the Pacific that we could see in the distance, it was like an army of leprechauns had scattered a thousand pots of gold into the water. We watched until the sun completely disappeared, leaving behind a sky of pink and lavender and blue. Eventually streetlights flickered to life.

For almost two hours we talked. I learned that Flynn was almost twenty-nine and had been engaged when he was twenty-four to a woman named Bridgett. "She came to live with her aunt in Stornoway and we hit it off right away."

"What happened?"

"She thought Stornoway was boring. She complained about it a lot and finally said if I wanted to marry her, we'd have to move to Glasgow 'cause Stornoway was eatin' her alive. I told her I wouldn't leave and she was gone within a week."

"That must have been hard."

"Aye. If she loved me it shouldn't have been so easy to leave. But so it is."

"Did she get married right away?"

Flynn laughed. "I don't think so. I guess I'm not as

skilled as you are."

We had moved to the ground and were leaning against the trunk of a large tree. I pulled my knees up and hugged them, resting my head on them as I looked at Flynn. "Are there very many girls for you to date?"

Flynn smiled. "Not many. I guess I have too few options and you have too many." I turned my head and looked out across the road.

"They say it only takes one if it's the right one," I said.

"Aye. And we've neither one found the right one."

"What if there isn't a right one?" I said it quietly, more to myself.

Flynn put his hand on my back. "Don't worry, Charlotte. There's a right one."

A ridiculous tear slid down my cheek. I hated that my emotions were still so close to the surface. I quickly brushed it away, hoping he hadn't noticed.

Flynn moved his hand from my back and pulled me into his side. I leaned my head on his shoulder. His hand was warm on my arm. "Don't be sad, Charlotte."

I swallowed hard. "I try not to be, but sometimes it's hard."

And then we just sat there. I should have felt foolish, but Flynn's arm around me felt kind and comforting.

After a while, my phone vibrated. It was Angus telling us he was almost to the park.

Flynn pulled me to my feet and we walked to the road to meet Angus.

Chapter 9

There was a short debate about who should sit where before I finally prevailed and Flynn sat in front with Angus. I wanted him to have more leg room after being crammed in my little car most of the day.

I sat behind Angus but stretched my legs across the width of the car. As nice as it was to have a car that easily fit in our tiny garage, I wondered if maybe I should trade the bug in for something larger. My legs were grateful for the extra space.

"You're a life saver," I said to Angus as he pulled away from the curb.

"Mighty nice of ya to drive down to get us," said Flynn.

"Couldn't leave Chuck stranded."

"Chuck?" asked Flynn.

I shook my head while Angus gave Flynn a rundown of my nicknames. Of course he didn't mention the nickname Flynn already knew.

"I can bring you down to get your car Saturday morning," Angus said.

"What about work? I'm sure I can get Will or Dad to bring me down."

"I don't mind. I don't work until Saturday evening. Sounds like as good a way to spend the day as anything."

The guys got along surprisingly well. I picked up bits and pieces of a lengthy conversation about golf as I dozed in and out. They talked about the downfall of Tiger Woods and where they would most like to golf.

"I told Bruce I wanted to golf Pebble Beach when I came, but he's been tied up during the week and there's a tournament there this weekend."

"I've always wanted to golf there myself. Crazy that I live this close and I've never done it."

"If I come back, we should do it," Flynn said.

"Sounds good."

"Charlotte can join us." Flynn turned around and smiled.

Angus looked at me in the rear-view mirror. "Charlotte's not much of a golfer."

"He's right. I couldn't justify spending that kind of money when I'm so bad. Besides, I would just ruin it for you guys that actually golf."

We took Flynn home first. The whole drop-off was awkward. I didn't really want to stand outside Angus's car and say goodbye, but Angus had to be exhausted and I didn't want to leave him sitting in the car while I walked Flynn to the door of his brother's condo.

I paused and we talked for a minute as I moved from the back seat to the passenger seat.

"We good for tomorrow?" Flynn asked. "I'll have Bruce's car."

"Maybe you can break his car too."

"Good way to leave my mark here in America, right? Pick you up at six?"

"Sure."

"I'll text ya for the address." We stood there, looking at each other awkwardly for a few seconds too long before Flynn took a few steps backwards. "Thanks, Charlotte. Sorry about your car."

"It's okay."

"It was a splendid day."

"Yeah. It was. Thank you."

"'Til tomorrow." He acted like he was tipping a hat that wasn't there.

"Bye."

I watched as Flynn went inside Bruce's building.

Angus was quiet when I got in the car. We drove several blocks before either of us spoke.

"Are you excited for tomorrow night?" I finally asked.

"Should be fun."

"I know you're going to like her. Aleena's amazing."

Angus nodded. He was so quiet.

"You must be so tired," I said.

"Yeah. It's been a long couple of days."

"Thanks again for coming to our rescue. I'm sorry you're not already in bed asleep."

"No problem."

And then it was quiet again. We were almost to my apartment before either of us spoke.

"Flynn seems like a nice guy."

"He is. Really nice."

"So you like him?"

"I guess so. But he's from Scotland."

"Scotland is probably a pretty nice place."

I laughed. "I'm sure it is."

"What if he's the one?"

I looked at Angus, trying to read his face. The way he said "the one" surprised me. Did he sound bitter? He kept his eyes on the road in front of us, his face as expressionless as I had ever seen it.

"Is it too much to hope that 'the one' lives in the same country as me?"

Angus shrugged. "It just seems like you've always been willing to give guys a chance, so why not this guy?"

There was an edge to Angus's voice I wasn't used to. If I didn't know him better I would have thought he was trying to pick a fight. "Are you trying to get rid of me?"

"I just don't want you to miss out on true love." And there was that tone again as he said "true love."

"Well, he's not 'the one.'"

"It seems like he likes you."

"No, he doesn't. Not like that. And there's no way I want to move halfway around the world. He doesn't want to move to America, either."

"I'm just saying he seemed interested."

"He knows I'm not looking for anything serious."

"How does he know?"

"I told him."

"You're a cold one." I stared at Angus. Was he joking? Or was he being so harsh because he was tired? I decided to ignore his thoughtless comment. He had driven all the way down to Carmel to rescue us, after all.

Angus pulled up to the curb in front of my apartment. I had never felt so ill-at-ease with him before. It felt like we had just argued and needed to make up, but that was ridiculous. I settled on, "Thank you again. I really appreciate you coming for us."

Angus shrugged. "You're welcome."

"Have fun tomorrow."

"You too."

As soon as I was inside, Angus pulled away. Neither of us had mentioned driving me to Carmel on Saturday. After the stilted conversation, I wasn't sure if Angus would want to or if I should try to make arrangements with someone else.

We were still two blocks away from Fort Mason Center, but already we could hear the music. Tonight it was jazz. I would have preferred one of the singer songwriters I had heard perform before, but even jazz sounds good live.

It was impossible to distinguish each individual aroma, but everything combined melded into a hunger monster that made me want to eat something from every truck.

Off the Grid is like a county fair and an episode of Top Chef combined. I had been to Off the Grid several times and had never been disappointed. Dozens of tables were set up in the parking lot, with more than thirty food trucks parked around the perimeter, each offering their own specialty food.

"What are you hungry for?" Flynn asked as he looked around.

"Everything."

"Then we'd better get started."

People were everywhere. Every food truck had a line. The line at Bacon, Bacon, and More Bacon was at least twenty people long. Paella for People had already sold out and all that remained was their mouthwatering picture.

It took about an hour, but by the time we were finished, we had shared a Say Cheese apple and cheddar grilled cheese sandwich, an Emilio's tamale, Your French Chef's sausages, Happy Dumplings potstickers, a Pie in the Sky chicken pot pie, candied bacon from Bacon, Bacon, and More Bacon, and Cream of the Crop's chocolate crème brulee.

"I think my eyes were bigger than my stomach," Flynn said. We were sitting at a table across from the band and had just finished our dessert.

"I know. I always say I'm not going to get carried away next time, but then I do."

"I just wanted to try everything since I may never get to come again," Flynn said.

"What's my excuse? I should come every week and limit myself to two trucks."

"How would you choose?"

"I know, that's the problem."

"I need to walk some of this off."

"Good idea," I said, scooting away from the table.

We walked from Fort Mason Center down Marina Boulevard. A few sailboats drifted out in the harbor, enjoying the breezy evening.

"Was it an American girl Bruce followed to San Francisco?"

"Aye. Her grandmother lived in Stornoway. She came to stay for a while after her grandmother broke her hip. Bruce had just finished at University and they met over the summer. He fell hard."

"Did she? Fall for him, I mean."

"I don't know. Seems she liked him. She told him he should come to San Francisco, so he did. Broke Jessie's heart. And then Kendra broke his."

"Sounds like a lot of broken hearts," I said.

"Not many people get through it all without one."

"There's too much heartbreak. Why can't we just find the right one and skip all the pain?"

"That'd be easier. But you wouldn't be the same Charlotte if you'd never had your heart broken. None of us would be the same."

"So Jessie liked Bruce?"

"Since primary school. He liked her too, until that summer. But then he followed Kendra to San Francisco and never came back."

"Maybe Jessie should have followed Bruce. Helped mend his broken heart."

Flynn laughed. "I don't think Jessie would ever move from the Isle."

The lights on the Golden Gate Bridge glowed in the distance.

"That's quite a sight," Flynn said.

"When I was in high school, we walked across the bridge for a fund-raiser. A boy a couple of years older than me got paralyzed in a car accident and someone organized a walk-the-bridge thing to raise money for a wheelchair that could be operated by barely moving your hand, or something. I'll never walk across the bridge again. It's a lot higher than it looks and it was so windy. I was a little freaked out."

"Charlotte's afraid of heights?" Flynn's tone was teasing.

"A little."

Flynn arched his eyebrows.

"Okay, more than a little. But I think it's justified." I told Flynn about my disastrous hot air balloon ride.

He nodded. "Are you going to conquer your fear by taking another ride?"

"No way."

Flynn laughed. "I guess we're all afraid of something."

"What are you afraid of?"

"Who said I was afraid?"

"You just said we're all afraid of something."

"I was just trying to make you feel better." Flynn nudged me with his elbow.

I laughed. "You just don't want to tell me."

"Aye. That's true."

"So what is it?"

"It's crazy." Flynn said, shaking his head.

"Come on. Tell me. I promise I won't laugh."

"Aye, but you will. You won't be able to help yourself."

"Try me."

"What was your favorite part of dinner?"

"No way. You're not changing the subject. Just tell

me and get it over with."

Flynn let out an exaggerated sigh. "Berries."

I giggled. "Did you say berries?"

Flynn pointed at me. "You lied. You said you wouldn't laugh."

I bit the sides of my mouth. "I'm not laughing."

Flynn shook his head. "I won't trust you again."

"Did you really say berries?"

Flynn nodded. "I guess berries can be pretty scary," I said turning my head away from him so he couldn't see the struggle I was having.

"You're a mean, mean girl, Charlotte."

"What kind of berries are the scariest?"

"Never trust a lass with a secret."

"I'm sorry. You just seem too big and strong to be afraid of berries."

"When I was five and Bruce was seven, he and his friends dared me to drip the juice from a Yew berry on my tongue."

"I've never heard of Yew berries."

"The juice isn't poisonous, but the seeds are, so you have to be very careful. I wanted Bruce and his friends to think I was as clever as they were, so I dripped the juice on my tongue. When we got home, I told Mum what I'd done and she nearly keeled over dead from fright. I told her I hadn't eaten a seed, but she made me drink Syrup of Ipecac until I'd thrown up again and again just to be safe. Ever since then, I've stayed away from berries."

"All berries?"

"Aye."

"But all berries aren't poisonous."

Flynn shrugged.

"How sad. You're missing out on so many delicious things."

"That's what I've heard, but have you tasted Syrup of Ipecac?"

"I don't think so."

"Nothing's worth the risk of having to drink that potion. It's the devil's drink."

I grabbed Flynn's arm. "Oh my gosh, you're in luck."

"What are you talking about?"

I let go of his arm and nodded at the sidewalk ahead of us. "Don't stare, but look at what's walking toward us."

Not far away was a fresh-off-the-ranch cowboy. At least that's what he looked like. His boots made a staccato sound on the sidewalk. His hat looked gray, and his giant belt buckle sparkled, even in the twilight.

"Evenin'," he said as he walked by.

Flynn turned around to watch the man after he passed us. "Now that's America."

I rolled my eyes. "Your trip has been a success."

"Do you think he was from Texas?" Flynn asked.

I laughed. "Or California."

It was almost eleven when Flynn pulled up to the curb at my apartment. He was in a loading only zone, but he didn't pay any attention. He turned off the car and met me on the sidewalk.

"Thanks for being my California tour guide," he said.

"You're welcome. I've had fun. This was good for me."

We stood by the wrought iron door that led inside, but I waited to reach for my key.

"You know, I think if I lived here or you lived in Stornoway, I'd try to put your nickname to rest."

My eyes settled on his feet. "I would probably let you try."

Flynn lifted my chin so we were looking at each other. His eyes were kind and a little smile played at the sides of his mouth. "Barmy Atlantic Ocean."

I wasn't sure what he was saying, but it didn't matter. I smiled. "Thanks for helping take my mind off things."

Flynn leaned against the wall like we had all night to stand out here talking, like his car wasn't at risk of a ticket or a boot. "Ya know what might really get your mind off things?"

I leaned against my gate facing him. "What's that?"

"A trip to somewhere far, far away from here." He swept his hand in a broad gesture that was probably meant to take in my neighborhood, the whole bay area, and possibly even the entire United States. "I know a great place that's known for takin' away your worries."

"And I'll bet you live there."

Flynn shrugged. "I do."

"Who knows? Maybe I will," I said, even though I knew it would never happen.

"I hope ya do."

And then Flynn leaned forward and kissed me. It wasn't a quick movement, so it shouldn't have taken me by surprise as much as it did. He just leaned forward until his lips were on mine. It wasn't like any kiss I had ever had. His lips weren't tentative or demanding. It wasn't a passionate declaration, but it wasn't a friendly peck, either. After a couple of seconds, he pulled away.

"Bye for now, Charlotte."

My fingers touched my lips as I watched him walk to his car. He smiled over the top of it and gave me a little wave, and then he was gone.

Chapter 10

"How did it go last night?" I asked as soon as I was in the car.

"Hi to you, too, Charlotte," Angus said.

"Sorry. Hi. I'm just dying to know how it went last night. Isn't Aleena great?"

Angus pulled out into traffic before he spoke. "She's really nice. And very pretty."

"What did you do?"

"We started the night at Off the Grid."

"You did? We were there last night, too. I didn't see you."

"You and your Scotsman?"

I let out an annoyed puff of air. "He's not mine. When were you there?"

"Early. About six."

"That's why we didn't see you. We went later. So what did you do after that?"

"We went to a movie."

"A movie? You can't talk at a movie."

"Don't worry, Charles. We had plenty of time

100

to talk."

"You did?"

"We went to Marigold's for dessert and ended up talking until about two this morning." Marigold's was an all-night diner a few blocks from Aleena's apartment.

"Please tell me you had the chocolate chip cookie pie with ice cream."

Angus laughed. "Sorry. I had the apple pie."

I sighed and shook my head. "Amateur."

"Don't worry. Aleena had the chocolate chip pie."

"Whew! I needed at least one of you to have had it."

"I'm pretty sure she enjoyed it. She said she was eating it in your honor since you set us up."

"You talked 'til two?" No wonder Aleena hadn't called last night like she had promised. Angus nodded. "You must have really hit it off."

"I guess we did."

"Are you going out again?"

"I invited her to come with us today, but she'd promised her mom she would help her find a dress for her cousin's wedding, so I'm meeting her for an early dinner before I have to be at the hospital."

"Wow. That's great."

The overcast sky sprung a leak about the time we hit the Pacific Coast Highway and I was glad we'd had better weather the day Flynn and I had driven down the coast.

"I was thinking we could get lunch at The Flying Fish Grill while we're down here." I said. "My treat to thank you for driving." We had eaten at The Flying Fish Grill when we were in college and a group of us had driven to Los Angeles for a concert. The next morning, we had decided to take the Pacific Coast Highway home instead of I-5. It was at The Flying Fish Grill that Will had discovered he liked oysters. He'd had to eat them because he lost a bet with Angus about the elevation of Mount Lyell in Yosemite. Will would eventually learn that when it came to silly trivia, he should never doubt Angus.

"Sorry. I'd better not. I've got a few things I need to get done before this next four-day shift, and I need to squeeze them in before I meet Aleena."

"Oh. Okay."

I have to admit I was disappointed. I had been excited to hang out for a little while with Angus. Except for therapy, we hadn't seen much of each other lately and I missed him. And I'd been craving tempura prawns. "When are you seeing Finn again?"

"It's Flynn, and probably never."

"He's gone home?"

"He goes home tomorrow. He's spending the weekend with his brother."

"Is he coming back?"

"Not that I know of."

"Are you going to Scotland to see him?" Angus said "Scotland" with a terrible British accent.

"No."

"So what was this exactly?"

"This was me being friendly and showing him around. And getting my head wrapped around the idea of dating again."

Angus shook his head. "Wow. I must have misread the signals the other night."

"What signals?"

"I don't know. It just seemed like he liked you."

"He did like me. Just not the way you're thinking."

"Whatever you say."

"What? You think it's not possible that a guy would want to be friends with me?"

"Whoa. Slow down, Chuckers. I'm a guy and I've been friends with you forever, so I'm obviously not saying that. I'm saying if I'd had to guess the other night, Flynn would have been happy with a little more than friends."

"Sorry to disappoint you, but we're just friends. I kept him company while his brother worked."

"Why would that disappoint me?" I didn't respond, and after a minute he said, "Did he kiss you?"

I sighed. "What are you doing, Angus?"

"Just trying to sort out exactly what's going on with you." His voice was flippant and had an edge.

I shook my head and looked out the passenger window at the water. What was going on with Angus and me? We had been friends for years and it seemed we'd been on the verge of fighting more the last week than we had in the last decade.

"So did he?"

"Sort of."

"It wasn't a 'sort of' question. Either he kissed you or he didn't."

"Yeah. He did. But it wasn't a big deal."

"Since when?"

"What?" The word came out sharper than I had intended, but this whole conversation had a sharp edge to it.

We passed a sign that said Carmel was thirty-two

miles away. I needed it to be closer than that.

"Since when is a kiss not a big deal to you? Has our little Charlotte started giving out kisses that don't mean anything?"

"Knock it off."

"I guess I've touched a little nerve."

"What's your deal, Angus?"

"I don't have a deal. I'm just used to you being honest with me, and I don't think you have been for a while now."

"How have I not been honest? I tell you everything. You want to know about the kiss? Fine, I'll tell you. He kissed me when he said goodbye. It completely took me by surprise and I have no idea what I even think about it. But it doesn't matter, because he's headed to Scotland tomorrow. And in a couple of months, I'll run into his brother or I'll get an email telling me he's getting married and it won't matter if he liked me or if he kissed me or if I liked him. None of it will matter. So there you go. I've been honest with you. And dang you, Angus, now I'm crying and I don't even know why."

I reached in my purse for a tissue, and when I came up empty, I started searching Angus's car. I found a napkin in the glove box. I wiped my eyes and blew my nose and then stuffed the napkin into my jacket pocket.

We drove in silence for several miles. I pulled the napkin out to dry my eyes a couple of times. I didn't even know exactly why I was crying. Was I this torn up about Flynn leaving? Was I still sad about Kyle and Wyatt? Was it because I was fighting with my best friend?

Or was it because with every guy I dated, the hope I had of finding love died a little more? Right now that hope was on life support, and I felt like if I wasn't careful, I would bump the cord and unplug it for good. I fidgeted with the drawstring on the bottom of my jacket, wishing I was already in my own car.

"I'm sorry, Charlotte." Angus's voice was quiet, and he put his hand over mine, holding it still. "I didn't mean to go off on you."

I held perfectly still for several seconds before I turned my hand over and clasped his. I don't think Angus and I had ever held hands before, and I was surprised how strong and comforting it felt.

"I know things have been hard, and I shouldn't have piled on. I'm sorry."

I nodded.

We held each other's hands until we pulled into Carmel. It was like our hands were somehow symbolizing our friendship and I needed to hold on tightly so it wouldn't slip away. I had lost so much. I couldn't lose Angus, too.

My car was sitting in front of the garage when we arrived. Angus pulled in beside it, put his car in park and turned to me.

"You okay?"

"I'll be fine." I attempted a smile.

"I know you will be. You always are."

I felt sad that my friend, someone who knew me as well as almost anyone, couldn't see that I wasn't fine.

I paid for the repairs and soon we were driving back toward San Francisco. I was hungry and tired and my mood was despondent. It took about two minutes of flipping through talk radio and obnoxious pop music, all with that infuriating buzz in the background, before I decided that as miserable as my thoughts were, they were better than the radio.

One week ago, I had spent the weekend crying in my bedroom. I knew I was perilously close to spending another weekend in the same condition.

Maybe I should go see Flynn. I was pretty sure he would be happy to see me. I wouldn't want to keep him from spending time with Bruce, but maybe I could join them.

I spent several minutes figuring out what I could say that would sound natural and friendly instead of pathetic and needy. Finally, I realized there was nothing I could say. I was not this desperate.

I picked up my phone and hit Angus's speed-dial button. I watched in the rear-view mirror as he put his phone to his ear.

"I'm going to turn off and go to Will and Gina's."

"Sounds fun. Tell them hi."

"I will. Thanks again for the ride. Have fun with Aleena."

"I will."

"Okay, see ya."

"Hey, Charlotte?"

"Yeah?"

There was a long pause and I thought we had been disconnected.

"Take care of yourself."

"Okay."

I was surprised to realize that today had been one of the worst days in recent memory. That didn't usually happen with Angus. I really needed to see family. I couldn't wait to snuggle up with sweet little Emily. Maybe I could rock us both to sleep and I wouldn't wake up until my life was somehow better.

I heard Mia's key in the apartment door and stepped into the hall to meet her.

"Hey," she said in a tired voice when she saw me.

"Wow. You look amazing. Where have you been?" She was wearing a ruffled navy blouse and an orange floral pencil skirt. Her hair was pulled up and she looked beautiful.

"I had a date."

I pulled out my phone. "Home before ten? Must not have been a very good date."

Mia shook her head, threw her purse on a chair, and headed for the kitchen. I sat on the couch to wait, and a minute later she joined me with a glass of water.

"Dating is a waste of time."

"That good, huh?"

"We went to Quince, which was nice."

"So the guy's not hurting for money. Was it good?"

"The food was great. But he was so boring. All he talked about was his job and model cars."

"Model cars?"

"Yeah. He makes little model cars and enters them into contests. Last year he won the model car Olympics or something." She smiled weakly. "I kinda zoned out when he started talking about the best kind of model glue and what color his winning car was."

I mustered a half smile. "At least we're starting to date. We've both been on a dry spell."

"I think this was my first and last date for a while. I just don't have the energy to work this hard for something so unfulfilling."

I reached across the couch and squeezed Mia's hand. She scooted over by me and leaned her head on my shoulder. "You're amazing, Charlotte. You just keep trying and trying, even when it doesn't work out. I just don't think I have it in me."

"I'm not amazing. I think my tank's about empty, too."

"We'll just live here until we're old and everyone will call us the stylish old maids and they'll wonder why we never married since we look so good and we're so accomplished and intelligent and witty," Mia said. "It'll be so mysterious."

"Or they'll think we're pathetic. Maybe we should be looking for a couple of cats to breed. We need to have cats all over the furniture and sitting in the window sills."

"I'm allergic to cats."

"Well, another dream to fall short on."

Mia laughed. "Did you get your car?"

"Yeah. And then I went to Will and Gina's. I held Emily all afternoon. I know I'm biased, but she's seriously the prettiest baby in the world."

"Hopefully McKayla won't have an ugly baby. The comparisons would be tragic." McKayla, my younger sister, and her husband, Connor, were having a baby the end of the summer.

"With Connor and McKayla as the parents, there's no way they'll have an ugly baby. Will and Gina are going to let me babysit next month while they get away for their anniversary. I can't wait."

My phone vibrated in my pocket. It was Aleena.

Aleena: Lunch. Monday. I'm paying 'cause boy do I owe you.

I groaned even though I should have been happy someone's love life was going better than ours.

"Bad news?" Mia asked.

"Depends on who you're asking."

Aleena got held up at work so lunch didn't happen on Monday. A gushing phone call took its place, with Aleena telling me how great Angus was and how glad she was I had set them up.

"Why haven't you ever gone after him?" she asked.

"Because he's Angus."

"Whatever. I'm not complaining."

Wednesday I got a text from Bruce's number telling me to check my Facebook page. When I did, I found a new friend request from Flynn Macgruger. Of course I accepted it. There was also a message.

Hi Charlotte,

Made it home. Mum and Jessie did a good job. Everything at the store was in order.

Bruce suggested I open a Facebook account. Said it would be easier to talk to you through it, so I did. I'm not sure how good it is for my ego, though. If you accept this, I'll have one friend. What does that say about me?

Hope you've caught up from the work you missed. Thanks again.

Flynn

I laughed when I looked at Flynn's Facebook page. There was nothing there. His profile picture was the stock silhouette. I was, indeed, his only friend. He had no history at all.

Hi Flynn,

Glad you arrived home safely. I never got behind while you were here, so work is fine.

If you'll notice, I have less than 50 friends and I've been on Facebook for four years. Sort of. I've never done much on here, although I do have an actual profile picture. You should consider adding one of those.

I just looked up what time it is in Stornoway and you're 8 hours ahead of us. That means you're probably already asleep and I'll be sleeping when you get up, fyi.

I can't believe I just used an acronym. I'd go back and change it but since you're new to Facebook, you should probably brush up on these. So here's a little lesson.

fyi – for your information

gtg – got to go

cu – see you

btw – by the way

rofl – rolling on the floor laughing

L8R – later

aad – acronyms are dumb

Yeah, I just made up that last one.

Have a great day.

Charlotte

I think I checked my Facebook page more that next twenty-four hours than I had during the last year. On Thursday, I found that Flynn had added a profile picture. It was one I took of him at Big Sur. He had also left a message.

Thanks for being my only friend. The time difference is inconvenient but we can work with it. Will you be around Saturday morning? Maybe around ten your time?

Flynn

I responded.

It's an appointment.

Chapter 11

Saturday morning I folded a load of laundry with my laptop open on the couch. I felt a little anxious. What did it mean that we were talking? I couldn't pass this off as being friendly to an out-of-towner because we were both at home. Did this mean we were going to be real friends? Where was Flynn's head in all this? Had that kiss meant something to him? Did I want it to mean anything? What if we didn't have anything to talk about?

A couple of minutes after ten, my computer rang like an old-fashioned telephone, and a message popped up telling me Flynn Macgruger would like to Skype. I accepted, and a few moments later, there was Flynn, filling my computer screen.

I settled into a corner of the couch to talk.

"Charlotte." That was a good way to start off.

"Hi."

And then we sat there looking at each other for several seconds before Flynn laughed. "I think we're supposed to talk."

I laughed too. "Yeah, I think we are. You look

the same."

What a ridiculous thing to say. What did I expect? Did I think that because he was in Scotland he would look somehow different?

Flynn laughed. "Can you believe it? I haven't aged much or anything."

I laughed at my silliness. "So what shall we talk about?"

"Did you get your car?"

I really didn't want to remember or talk about the trip back to Carmel to pick up my car. "Yep. It's running great now."

"That's good."

"How was your trip home?"

"Long. I had stops in Philadelphia and Glasgow. Every flight was crowded until the last one to Stornoway. I had two seats to myself on that one, but it only lasted an hour."

And then we were off. We talked easily for more than an hour. We talked about the hardware store and babysitting Emily and the mugs I was designing for Trees of Mystery.

After a while, Flynn said, "I've got to head over to Mum's. She's got a slow drain."

"Does she live close by?"

"I'll show ya." He picked up his computer and turned it around. Out Flynn's window, I could see the green countryside and a narrow country road. And then there was a little white house. It looked so picturesque.

"It's lovely there, isn't it?"

"The best part is behind our houses. Hang on."

Suddenly, the picture on my screen was just Flynn's blue, button down shirt, up close. Then I heard a door open and he turned the screen around. "This is what's behind our houses."

A stream, about five or six feet wide, ran behind Flynn's house. Behind the stream were green, rolling hills. "There's a footbridge over there," he said. He turned the computer to show me, but I couldn't see it. "Sometimes I sit back there and fish."

"It looks so peaceful."

"A little different than San Francisco."

Flynn turned the computer around, and his face was back on the screen.

"Maybe next time I'll take ya over to see Mum's house. That's where I grew up."

"You can show me the Isle of Lewis while I sit on my couch."

Flynn laughed. "I'd rather show ya in person."

"This was fun."

"Let's do it again," Flynn said.

"Smile."

Flynn had already been smiling, but once I said it, he straightened his features into a frown.

"Come on. Smile."

"What are you doing?"

"I was just going to take a screen shot. Come on. Pose for the camera."

"Ah, so ya don't forget what I look like." Flynn smiled again, and I snapped a picture.

"Thanks. Now go fix your Mum's drain."

"Talk to you later, Charlotte."

We talked several times over the next two weeks. Flynn showed me the rest of his house. I showed him some of my sketches. He tried to walk me to his mum's, but somewhere along the way, the connection gave out. He had shown me half the place before he realized I wasn't there.

"Are you outside?" Flynn asked. He was sitting in the office of the hardware store and I was in my parents' back yard. I hadn't seen my parents for a few weeks, so I had come home to spend the weekend. Mom and Dad had exchanged a look when I had said I was going to the deck to talk to Flynn. I could read the reservations on both of their faces.

"I'm at my mom and dad's house."

"You should introduce me," Flynn said.

"You haven't introduced me to your mom."

"I will if you want me to."

"She's probably not thrilled that you're talking to me."

"Why wouldn't she be?"

Suddenly, I felt silly and presumptuous. I knew my parents were hoping I wasn't falling for a man from Scotland and I had just figured his mom would have the same reservations, especially given her history with Bruce. But maybe Flynn had already assured her we were just friends.

"Do you really want to meet them?" I was anxious to leave the subject of Flynn's mom and my imagined concerns.

"Yaw."

"Just a minute."

I went in the house and found my parents washing dishes. "Can you come out here? Flynn would like to meet you."

"Meeting the parents has sure changed since I was your age." Dad said and smiled.

"I'm sure he's nice, Charlotte, but is there a reason for us to meet him?"

"Mom, we're friends." Mom dried her hands and followed Dad outside. I moved the laptop to the far side of the table so Mom and Dad would both fit in the screen. I stood behind them. "Flynn, this is my Dad and Mom. And this is Flynn."

Flynn flashed his best smile. "Nice to meet you, Charlotte's Mum and Dad."

"How are you, Flynn?" Dad asked.

"Very well. Just enjoying a visit with your daughter."

"Did you enjoy your stay in California?" Mom asked. I could tell she was trying to be friendly, despite her misgivings.

"Very much. Charlotte was kind enough to show me around. I had a grand time."

The four of us exchanged an awkward round of pleasantries and then Dad excused them to run a few errands. I felt relieved when they left. Skype probably wasn't the best way to introduce people.

Flynn seemed unfazed and immediately began another topic of conversation.

"I'm buildin' a guest house for the Crawfords."

"The Crawfords?"

"They live just outside Stornoway. Mr. Crawford taught me mathematics at my primary school, and now he's havin' me build a guest cottage."

"Is he planning on company?"

"He's building it for his son and daughter-in-law. They'll live there and take care of him."

"Why does he need taken care of?"

"He's not well. They'll live in the guest house until he dies and then his son will inherit the house. I'll be building it this summer."

"Congratulations. Another building job."

"I'm lookin' over plans with them right now and I'll get started as soon as they pick something. I like working the store, but truthfully, Charlotte, I'm excited to build. It makes me want to get up in the morning." I liked seeing his enthusiasm as he talked about the project. His eyes lit up and he sat on the edge of his chair.

"You'll have to show it to me as you build it."

Flynn took a deep breath. "Didn't you tell me you have plenty of vacation days saved up?"

"When did I say that?"

"When I was there. When I asked you to go with me to Big Sur."

I smiled, surprised he had remembered that.

"How many days do you have?"

"I'm not even sure. More than two weeks."

"You should come here."

"Flynn—"

"Just listen. You've got vacation days. I owe you a tour."

"You don't owe me anything."

"Shhh. I'd like to show you the Isle of Lewis. I'd like to show ya Stornoway. I'd even like to show ya Glasgow. Why don't ya come?"

"I can't just head off to Scotland by myself."

"Sure you can. And once the plane lands ya won't be by yourself."

"I don't know."

"If I bought you a plane ticket, would you come?"

"Don't you dare. How much would it even cost?"

Flynn told me what he had paid for his flight.

"Flynn, don't try to surprise me. That's too much, and I couldn't come if you did that."

"If ya want to come, we can split it if that'll make ya feel better." His eyes looked so eager, and he put his hands together in front of his face imploringly. "Charlotte, I'd like ya to come."

"I appreciate the offer, but if I ever decided to come, I would pay for the ticket myself."

A bell rang in the background.

"Flynn, what ya doing?" It was a woman's voice.

"Hi Jessie. I'm talking to Charlotte, the girl I met in San Francisco."

"Hi Charlotte." A pretty woman, probably in her mid-twenties, leaned over Flynn's shoulder and waved. She had windblown, blonde hair and dimples in her cheeks.

"Hi Jessie." I wondered what Flynn had told her about me.

"I'm just dropping off the mail. See ya later."

"So will ya come?" Flynn picked up the conversation like it had never been interrupted.

The invitation was tempting and I could use a vacation, although I wasn't sure I was comfortable with what accepting it might imply.

"I'll think about it."

I was watching The Travel Channel when I heard the garage door open. I knew Dad and Mom would have some questions, so I turned down the volume when they walked in.

"You through talking to your friend?" Mom asked.

"Yeah. It's getting late there."

Mom and Dad sat down. Neither of them spoke right away. Anyone looking at us would just have assumed that we were all terribly interested in the building of the world's largest cruise ship, but none of us were really watching it.

After a few minutes, I turned off the television. "You can ask me anything you want, and I'll do my best to answer you. I just need to warn you that I'm not sure I'll even know all the answers."

Mom let out a sigh and Dad spoke first. "Flynn seems like a nice man."

"He is. He's very kind and thoughtful."

"We're glad about that. You've been sad for a long time, and it's nice to see you smiling again. It's just . . ."

Mom picked up when Dad's voice trailed off. "Honey, have you thought about where this is going and what it will mean for you?"

"We just don't want you to get hurt again," Dad said.

I nodded. "I know. I don't think it's going anywhere, but I can't say that for sure."

Mom was holding her breath. I could see it. And her hands were clasped tightly in her lap. I moved over onto the couch with her and put my hand over hers. "Mom, you've got to breathe or you'll die."

Mom let out a choked breath and we all started laughing.

"Look at what you're doing to your mother," Dad said. "Are you trying to make me a widower?"

"If I'm doing this to Mom, imagine what I'm doing to myself," I said. I was glad the tension was broken and we could laugh.

"What are you doing to yourself?" Mom asked.

"I really don't know. I'm trying not to overthink everything. I've always planned and analyzed every detail and look where it's gotten me. Maybe it's time for me to quit thinking so hard and just let things happen."

"We don't disagree with you about that. It's probably good for you to relax a little and worry less, but when you talk about letting things happen . . ." Dad's voice trailed off again, but then he finished. "I guess we'd just be a little more comfortable if what was happening was happening with someone who lives in America."

"I know. I couldn't agree with you more. But just so you know, right now we're just friends. This may not go anywhere at all. Next week we might get sick of talking to each other and never speak again. I just don't know."

"What if he falls in love with you?" Mom asked.

"Oh, Mom. Don't you get it? Most guys don't fall in love with me. We date and then they fall in love with someone else."

"Charlotte, that's not true. You've had plenty of guys who have fallen for you."

"The only one I know for sure is Kyle. And he was so head over heels that it took him less than six months to get engaged to someone else. It's not likely Flynn is going to fall madly in love with me. We're just friends. In fact, he probably feels sorry for me."

"Why would he feel sorry for you?" Mom asked.

"Because I told him everything. I even warned him that if he dates me, he'd better be ready to get married. He told me he's going to be the one that breaks my curse."

Mom shook her head. "Your curse. I don't even know that it's true."

"How can you doubt it's true? It's happened with every single guy, and I'm so sick of it."

Dad looked thoughtful for a moment. "You're a smart girl, Charlotte, and we certainly don't know what your future is supposed to be. Just be careful. Take things slowly."

"And if you and this man fall in love, please have him move here," Mom said.

Chapter 12

I pulled into the parking lot at The Women's Center. McKayla's Subaru was already in the lot, so I hurried into Dr. Hapshaw's office. McKayla put down a magazine when she saw me and pointed at a chair next to her.

"I hope they call me soon. I might have an accident in their chair if they make me wait too long."

"I was worried you might have gone in without me. I didn't know there was so much road construction on the way out here."

Today was McKayla's ultrasound. She had asked me to come with her since Connor was out of town.

"Thanks for driving out."

"Are you kidding? I'm sorry Connor couldn't come with you, but I'm thrilled to be here. Are you finding out what it is?"

McKayla scrunched up her face. "I think so."

"You think so?"

"Connor left it up to me, and I keep going back and forth. Part of me wants to know so I can plan, but being surprised would be so much fun."

I hmphed. "So you can plan? Give me a break. This is me here, remember? You can tell everyone else you want to know so you can plan, but I know you just have no patience. Zero. That's why you'll find out."

McKayla giggled and then squirmed in her chair. "Don't make me laugh. Please tell them to call my name. I'm dying here."

"Do you hope it's a boy or a girl?"

"I don't care at all. Do you think we should find out or be surprised?"

I shook my head. "I'm not making the call. That's up to you guys."

"Which means it's up to me. I'm sure everyone thinks I'll find out."

"Everyone who knows you." I jostled her with my elbow.

"McKayla Ward? We're ready for you."

"Thank goodness," McKayla said.

We followed the ultrasound technician to a room down the hall. She was about five feet tall with short, fiery red hair.

"I feel like an ogre," McKayla whispered.

"Good, you wore stretchy pants," said the technician, whose nametag read Poppy. Had her parents known she would have red hair?

McKayla giggled and we both looked at her. "I'm sorry. 'Stretchy pants' just sounded funny."

Poppy smiled and instructed McKayla what to do.

Soon we were watching the screen as Poppy showed us the baby's head and arms and legs.

"Do you want to know if it's a boy or girl?"

McKayla looked at me.

"I told you I'm not deciding."

She sighed. "No. I want to be surprised."

"Wow." I nodded.

"All right," said Poppy.

"Can you tell?" asked McKayla, and Poppy laughed.

"Yes, but I can keep it to myself."

"Oh never mind, just tell me."

"Are you sure?" Poppy and I said at the same time.

"No, no. Don't tell me."

"I'll tell you what. I'll write it down and put it in an envelope. That way you don't have to decide right now."

Poppy wrote down some measurements and snapped a couple of pictures before she told McKayla she could go to the bathroom. While McKayla was out of the room, Poppy wrote something on a paper and sealed it in the envelope. When she came back, Poppy handed her two photographs and the envelope.

"Congratulations. Your baby looks healthy and happy."

I followed McKayla to Su Casa, where we ate fish tacos. The sealed envelope sat on the table between us.

"It would shock everyone if I didn't find out, wouldn't it?" she asked.

"Just because it would be totally out of character."

"I feel like being surprised."

"Then throw it away."

"I don't know if I can."

We laughed.

"Mom says you were dating a guy from Scotland."

I rolled my eyes. "Dating is a strong word for it. We

went out a couple of times while he was here visiting his brother."

"Mom says you're still talking to him."

"We talk sometimes."

"Mom's worried you're going to fall in love and move to Scotland."

"What is with everyone? I'm not moving to Scotland."

"If you guys fall in love, he'll move here?"

"We're friends. We're not falling in love."

"So what's he like?"

"He's thoughtful and kind and good-looking, in a big, Scottish lumberjack sort of way."

McKayla's mood became serious. "I love you and I want you to be happy, but I don't think I could stand it if you moved to Scotland. I want my baby to know its Aunt Charlie."

I reached across the table and squeezed McKayla's hand. "Don't worry. I'm not moving anywhere."

McKayla squeezed back. "Good. Now do me a favor and go throw that in the garbage." She pointed at the envelope on the table.

"Are you sure?"

"Positive."

I picked up the envelope and walked to a combination ashtray and garbage can just outside the door. I glanced into the garbage and immediately knew if I threw it away, it would be there to stay. I looked through the glass door at McKayla as I held the envelope over the opening. When she smiled and nodded, I dropped it.

Will and Gina lived in a 1920s bungalow in Berkeley. They had bought it as a fixer-upper last year when Will got a job in the prosecutor's office. Their first fix had been the nursery. They had painted it lavender with white trim. In one corner, Gina had painted a white tree, its branches stretching across the wall above the crib. A white bird sat on a limb. All the furniture was white and an antique chandelier hung from the ceiling. It was the prettiest nursery I had ever seen.

Just before Gina gave birth to Emily, they'd had the kitchen renovated, knocking out a wall so it was bigger and brighter and opened onto a sitting area on the covered porch. This was my favorite part of the house.

"We've moved the tv out here," Will said. "You won't want to hang out in the living room. It's a disaster."

"Will's sanding the paint off all the woodwork in there."

"I still can't imagine why people painted over all that trim. Especially the beams."

"I'll bet that's a huge job," I said.

"I'm glad I didn't know how hard it would be or I might not have started it. It'll be worth it when it's finished."

"Charlotte, are you sure you're okay with this?" Gina asked as I took Emily from her arms. "She still doesn't sleep through the night."

"I'm not just okay with it. I've been living for this weekend ever since we first talked about it. You can't deny me now."

Gina giggled, but it sounded more nervous than happy.

"Everything will be fine," Will said and put his arm around Gina's shoulders. "Charlotte will take good care of her."

"I know. I know. I'm not doubting you, Charlotte." Her voice changed to baby talk. "I've just never left you overnight before, have I, little peanut?" She kissed Emily's chubby cheek half a dozen times.

"I promise we'll be fine. I've got both of your cell numbers. The doctor's number is on the fridge. Mom's less than an hour away. Everything's going to be great."

"Thanks, Charles." Will tugged on my ponytail as he walked by, pulling Gina behind him.

"I'll call and check in later tonight," Gina said as she firmly planted her feet and refused to move another inch until she had kissed Emily again.

When Will and Gina had first talked about going away for their anniversary, they had planned on a three-day weekend, but sometime in the last few weeks, they'd changed it to just Saturday to Sunday. Gina couldn't stand the thought of being away from Emily for more than one night. I was a little disappointed, but I understood.

"At least we've got all day today and all day tomorrow," I said to her as I fed her a bottle. She looked at me as she ate, pausing to give me a milky smile every few sips. She was charming.

A lasagna was baking in the oven, Emily was in her

bouncer on the kitchen table, and I was pulling a bag of salad out of the refrigerator when the doorbell rang.

It was Angus.

"Charles, what are you doing here?"

"I'm watching Emily while Will and Gina are in Eureka for their anniversary."

"Oh, I forgot that was this weekend. I'm just dropping off Will's GoPro."

"Cool. What did you film?"

"Aleena and I went mountain biking at McLaren."

"I didn't know Aleena was a mountain biker."

"It was her first time, but she did great." Angus handed me the camera bag.

"Hey, you should stay for lasagna. Gina left a whole pan."

"We were just headed out to dinner." Angus turned and pointed to his car at the curb. Aleena waved from the passenger seat and I waved back.

"Oh. I didn't know she was with you. You guys have fun."

"Unless," Angus looked from the car back to me. "I can check with Aleena and see if she wants to stick around and eat with you. If there's enough."

"There's plenty," I said. "But I don't want to ruin your plans."

"Let me talk to her."

Angus walked down the sidewalk and opened the car door to talk to Aleena. I don't know why I felt so awkward waiting there. This was Angus and Aleena. Two of my best friends in the world. But I had never been with them as a couple before, and it felt strange to have the two of them deciding together if they wanted to fit me into their evening. I wished I hadn't invited him. What if they said no? Would it feel like a double rejection?

Aleena got out of the car, and they walked to the house together. They looked adorable. Aleena was so tiny and cute next to Angus.

"Yay! You're staying," I said.

"Gina's lasagna is as good as anything we could go get," Angus said.

"And we might as well keep you company," said Aleena.

"The lasagna's got about twenty more minutes," I said. "That sounds like just the right amount of time for Angus to mix up some chocolate chip cookies."

"You bake?" Aleena asked.

"He makes great cookies."

"I'll help you," Aleena said.

Emily needed to be fed, so I held her and gave her a bottle while Angus and Aleena mixed up cookie dough. It was odd to watch them. I knew them so well individually, but watching them with each other felt like watching two strangers.

"Where are the cookie sheets?" Aleena asked.

"Above the refrigerator," I said.

Aleena used a stepstool to retrieve one. "Look. I'm as tall as you," she said.

Angus stepped closer. "No, I've still got you by a couple of inches."

"I don't think so." She moved her free hand between the top of her head and the top of his. "I don't know. Looks pretty even to me."

And then she put her hand behind his neck, pulled him closer, and kissed him. On the mouth.

"This is great. I can kiss you without getting a neck ache."

Suddenly, it was like an awkward bomb had detonated in the room. I wasn't sure why. Angus and Aleena were dating, so it shouldn't be strange that they acted like it. Angus looked at me. Aleena looked from Angus to me and back. I quickly looked at Emily.

"Oh my, you smell terrible," I said to Emily, even though all I could smell was the lasagna. "We'd better go change your diaper." I couldn't get out of the room fast enough.

I had been in Emily's room a couple of minutes when I heard the timer go off.

"Hey, Charles?" Angus called. "Do you want me to take this out?"

"Sure. I'll be there in a minute."

When I returned to the kitchen, the awkwardness had passed, and we sat down to Gina's delicious lasagna and a salad.

"Have you heard from Flynn?" Aleena asked between bites.

"We talked last night for a while."

"You're still talking to him?" Angus asked. He sounded surprised.

"They've been talking a lot," Aleena said.

"I don't know if I'd say 'a lot.'" I really didn't want to talk about this.

"I think he really likes Charlotte," Aleena said.

"We're friends."

"How much do you talk?" Angus asked.

"A couple of times a week, I guess."

"Maybe at the beginning it was a couple of times a week, but hasn't it picked up lately?" Aleena asked.

I shrugged and kept chewing, even though I had already swallowed.

"Have you seen that new Reese Witherspoon movie?" I asked.

"Nice try," Aleena said. "Let's talk about Scotland. When are you going?"

"I'm not," I said.

"You really should," Aleena said. "What a great chance to see another part of the world." Aleena turned to Angus. "He's invited her over and over and she keeps putting him off."

"Why?" Angus turned to me.

"I'm busy. I've got lots of projects going on at work."

"Oh please. That's not why you're not going."

I gave Aleena a pointed look, but she wasn't looking at me, so she didn't see it.

"Why aren't you going?" Angus asked.

I took another bite of salad. "I think she's not going because she's afraid she's falling for him and a boyfriend in Scotland is pretty inconvenient."

"I've never said I'm falling for him, but you're right. Scotland isn't convenient."

"Maybe he'll move back here," Angus said. "His brother did."

"And that's why he won't," I said. "He doesn't want to leave his mom and the family business."

"Maybe you could split your time between here and

131

there." Finally, Aleena looked at me and I gave her a "shut up" look. "What? I'm just trying to help you work things out. Maybe the fortune meant long-term romance."

"What fortune?" Angus asked.

"Charlotte's fortune cookie that said 'romance will come to you from foreign lands,'" Aleena said.

"First of all," I said, "that was *your* fortune. Second, I don't believe in fortunes. Third, let's talk about something else."

"Why?" Angus asked. "He seemed like a nice guy."

I sighed. "He is a nice guy. A nice guy who lives in Scotland."

"Who's invited you to come visit," Aleena said.

"I think you should go," said Angus. I stared at him. When I realized my mouth was hanging open, I hurried and clamped it shut. "What?" Angus looked at my surprised face. "Has he asked you to marry him and move there forever?"

I shook my head. For some reason, I had expected Angus to discourage me from going. I would have thought he would disapprove. I'd have imagined him saying, "Don't follow a guy halfway around the world unless you mean business." But instead he was telling me I should go.

Angus and I looked at each other for longer than was comfortable. I could feel Aleena's eyes on us, and I wanted to look away, but I needed to read what was behind Angus's words. Finally, he lowered his eyes. "Just go. There's nothing here to stop you."

What did he mean? My family was here. My friends were here. My job was here. There was plenty here to stop me.

132

I laughed, but it sounded fake. "If I didn't know better, I'd say you want me to move to another country."

Angus shrugged. "Just want you to be happy, Charlotte, and you don't seem to be happy with what you've got here."

I took a drink of water and blinked hard, determined not to cry.

I think Aleena sensed the need to change the subject, because she piped in with a funny story about one of the waiters at work. We all laughed, but it didn't feel like friends laughing. It felt forced and tense.

When they had first agreed to stay, I had thought maybe we could watch a movie or play games after dinner, but now I just wanted them to go. "I've got these dishes," I said when we were finished eating.

"We can help you," Aleena said.

"No." It came out a little more forcefully than I had meant for it to. "Really. You guys had plans, and I've already interrupted them enough."

"If we go now we can probably make a movie," Angus said.

"What about the cookies?" Aleena asked.

"Charlotte, do you mind if we split the dough and take some with us?" I didn't need to answer because Angus was already dividing it.

"Here," I said, handing him a freezer bag.

Aleena looked confused as we divided the dough. I didn't look at Angus and I'm pretty sure he was avoiding me, too.

"Thanks for dinner," Angus said at the door. "Tell Gina the lasagna was delicious. And be sure Will sees I brought back the GoPro. I don't want him thinking I still have it."

"I'll tell them," I said.

Aleena hugged me goodbye and followed Angus down the sidewalk to the car. I felt a flood of relief when they pulled away and turned the corner.

And then I felt abandoned. I had just spent time with my two closest friends, and I felt utterly alone.

Emily began crying and I was grateful to hear it. Maybe caring for her would keep me from analyzing what had just happened.

Chapter 13

*C*uddy was just finishing up a haircut when I stopped into his shop. He had owned the barbershop just below my apartment for more than forty years and he was one of my favorite things about where I live.

"Charlotte. Sit down. I'm nearly finished and then I've got a break for a few minutes."

I put my bag of groceries on the counter and sat down in one of Cuddy's three barber chairs. A man who looked to be in his late twenties or early thirties sat in another chair. Cuddy's gnarled hands worked quickly, shaving the man's neck. He brushed off the loose hair and squeezed a dab of Brylcreem, rubbing his hands together and then working it into the short strands. Then Cuddy worked his magic with a comb, and the man looked ready for a walk down the red carpet. Cuddy led him to the cash register and took his payment before shaking the man's hand.

I liked watching Cuddy work. Despite his age, his carriage was tall and elegant and he was a perfect gentleman.

When the customer was gone, Cuddy turned around and smiled at me. "Charlotte, this is a nice surprise. How are you?"

"I'm doing well. I just went grocery shopping, and when I saw these, I thought of you." I pulled out a package of Oreos. I knew Cuddy loved Oreos.

Not long after I had moved into my apartment, a bouquet of flowers had been left at Cuddy's Barbershop for me. It was a stunning arrangement of Juliet garden roses, and Cuddy had been excited for me to get home so he could give them to me. I had carried them upstairs in a perfumed euphoria, eager to open the card and see what the occasion was.

I had been dating Brad for about two months. It had been a casual relationship based on our mutual excitement to be college graduates. Brad's last name was Emell, which meant that during our college graduation ceremony, we were seated beside each other. We talked about our excitement to get out in the real world, and I coveted his long eyelashes. Just before we threw our caps, he had pulled out his cell phone and asked if he could have my number so he could give me a call. He seemed nice and I was feeling a little giddy about graduating, so giving him my number seemed like a good thing to do.

Brad landed an advertising job while we were dating and it crossed my mind that maybe this lavish bouquet was to celebrate his first full week on the job.

I put the flowers on the counter and pulled the card out of the little envelope.

Charlotte,

Thanks for helping me kill time while I waited for

Ashley to get home. It's been fun. Maybe I'll see you around.

Brad

What? This was the first time he had ever mentioned Ashley. If I'd had stronger feelings for Brad, I would have been disappointed. As it was, I was just incensed. I ran into Brad and Ashley at Bed, Bath and Beyond several months later. They were filling out their wedding registry. Brad introduced me as a girl from one of his classes, even though we had never been in a class together.

I still think of Brad as one of the biggest jerks I've dated.

The morning after the flower delivery, Cuddy stepped out of the barber shop and asked me what the occasion had been. I told him it was a very beautiful breakup bouquet. Later that day, when he closed up the shop, he rang my bell and said he had something for me. I went down to meet him, and he handed me a package of Oreos.

"These are my favorite. My wife, Belle, used to get these for me if I was having a hard day. I thought they might cheer you up."

I had hugged him and then opened the package right there on the doorstep and given him a few.

I love Cuddy.

"Oh, Charlotte, you don't have to buy me Oreos."

"Actually, I wanted a few but I didn't want a whole box, so you're saving me from myself."

"Well, let's get you a few."

Cuddy opened the package and I took three Oreos. "Thanks."

He shook his head. "Silly girl." He ate a cookie. "I wish I had a single grandson. I would like to make you part of my family." This wasn't the first time he had said this.

"We'll just pretend I'm your grand-daughter."

"I like that." He gave me a grand-fatherly smile.

The front door opened and two men entered the shop.

"I'd better get the rest of these groceries put away," I said.

Cuddy patted my back. "Thank you for the cookies."

The sun was blinding when I stepped back out on the sidewalk. I turned to my right to unlock my door, and there stood Kyle, ringing my doorbell. I had practically run into him, so there was no slinking away and hiding.

"Charlotte. Hi."

"Hi."

He looked good. So good. He wore a pair of gray chinos and a maroon Henley with the sleeves pushed up almost to his elbows. I looked down at my purse. I couldn't handle looking at his eyes. Or his smile. It occurred to me that as good as he looked, it might have been hard to live in the shadow of his dazzle.

"I hope you don't mind that I stopped by to see you."

"No. No. Not at all. Of course not." *Shut up, Charlotte.*

"Good. You've been on my mind and then I saw Jayne and Trent a couple of nights ago. I asked how you were doing, and she said I should ask you."

"She did?" I wasn't sure what Jayne was thinking. Was she respecting my privacy? Or did she think she could reignite what we had?

"Have you had lunch?"

I couldn't believe Kyle was standing here. I had wanted to see him for so long, and now that he was here, I didn't know what to do.

"Um ..."

"I just want to talk to you. Just an hour or so. Unless you've already eaten."

I shook my head. "I haven't. Let me go put these groceries away."

"Of course. I'll just wait down here. I thought we could walk to Anthony's and get a sandwich."

"I'll be back." My hand shook as I unlocked the door. I didn't hurry. I needed a few minutes to mend my nerves. I put the groceries away and took a minute to brush through my hair before I went back down. I stood inside the door for a minute, my hand on the knob, and took a few deep breaths.

"Ready?" Kyle asked.

"Sure."

The walk to Anthony's was as awkward as any walk I had ever taken. I left a couple of feet between us. The last thing I wanted was to accidentally touch him. Did he know I knew he was engaged? Would it be best to let him tell me and then congratulate him, or should I get it out there in the open? Would he act overjoyed or sheepish?

I wanted to turn around and walk back to my apartment.

When we arrived at the restaurant, Kyle held the door. I felt him glance at me while we waited in line to order our sandwiches, but I kept my eyes pinned on the menu board on the wall. After we ordered, we sat down at an empty booth to wait for our food, and I really looked at Kyle for the first time since he had startled me on the sidewalk. He was still handsome. His hair was a little shorter than it had been while we were dating. It was combed neatly in place and looked very polished.

"Congratulations," I said and smiled what I hoped was a genuine-looking smile.

"Thank you. I thought you probably knew, but I wasn't sure."

"I've known for a while."

I twisted my hands in my lap, glad he couldn't see them. They would certainly give away my flustered state of mind.

"Wyatt was wondering if Angus knows."

"He does."

Kyle nodded. "It was crazy how it came about. Mom had hired Wyatt to plan a Christmas reception at our house." I noticed that he said "reception" instead of "party." Maybe politicians don't have parties. "She was there at the house working with Mom when I stopped in one afternoon. We talked for a minute that day, but not much. Then she was there at the reception, working, and after it was over we went out for coffee and hit it off."

"I was surprised when I first found out, but after I thought about it, it seemed like a really good match. She'll be a good wife for you."

Kyle nodded again. "She's great."

A waiter brought our sandwiches to the table. I cut mine in half and took a bite.

"How have you been, Charlotte?"

I didn't tell him how much I had missed him. I didn't tell him how many times I had looked at his pictures or how many times I'd almost called him. I didn't tell him how many days I had spent crying or that, even now, it was hard to look at him without feeling the loss.

"I'm good."

"Are you dating anyone?" Kyle looked earnest and I knew if I said I was, it would assuage his guilty conscience. Not that Kyle had been at fault. I had initiated our breakup. But I knew there was probably some guilt that he had moved on so quickly. I've always been uncomfortable with the discomfort of others, and I didn't want Kyle to feel bad.

"I'm sort of seeing a guy from Scotland."

"Really? Wyatt was sure you'd be dating Angus."

"Why would I be dating Angus?"

Kyle shook his head. "Tell me about this guy from Scotland."

"Well, he's there. In Scotland. So I guess we're sort of attempting the long-distance thing."

"How did you meet?"

I gave Kyle a brief rundown on how we met and how we were still communicating, much to my surprise. "He keeps inviting me to Scotland to visit."

"Are you going?"

I sighed. "I'm not sure yet."

"Hmm," Kyle said, his brow furrowed.

"What?"

Kyle shrugged and waited a minute, considering his words. "It's just . . ." He wiped his mouth with his napkin. "I know I don't have any right to offer my opinion, but . . ."

"Just say what you're thinking."

Kyle rubbed the side of his face thoughtfully. "Just try not to let things go on too long if you're not sure you can live with the situation."

I stifled a gasp. He might as well have slapped me in the face. Did Kyle think I had let things go on too long with him? Did he think I'd led him on? I had been trying to convince myself I could make things work with the life he had chosen.

I wasn't sure what to say. I felt an impulse to defend myself, but I didn't want to relive our entire relationship. Especially the breakup.

"The situation?"

"You know. The whole long-distance thing. One of you leaving your family. Your country. It wouldn't be easy."

The conversation felt patronizing, but Kyle had always been too kind to talk down to me. He was probably concerned, and given our awkward circumstances, he was expressing himself as well as he could.

"I know how hard it would be. That's why I haven't agreed to go visit him. If I do, I know I'll have to make some hard choices. And I'll have to live with the consequences."

Kyle smiled kindly. "We've been through that."

I smiled back. "Yeah. We have."

"I probably should have told you about my plans a lot earlier. It might have made things easier on both of us."

I shrugged. "But if we'd broken up earlier, we might have missed out on some great times. And you might never have met Wyatt."

"That's true."

"Then I guess it was all worth it."

Kyle looked into my eyes. "You always were such a good sport. I really hope you end up with someone amazing."

I laughed under my breath. "Me too."

***

I spent the afternoon cleaning the apartment. Mia had gone to her parents for the weekend and I was glad. It gave me a chance to work and think and try to clear my head. I didn't turn on the television or any music. I needed to mull things over in my mind—both my surprising lunch with Kyle and my confusing feelings about Flynn.

Even though I had been bugged by the way Kyle had said it, I knew he was right. I needed to make a decision about Flynn. I liked talking to him. He had become a good friend. But I didn't know if I could ever move so far from everything I knew and loved. Of course, if I fell in love with Flynn, I wouldn't be leaving everything I loved. I'd just be leaving almost everything, but I would have him.

I took out my frustration on the tub and toilet, and by the time I was finished, the bathroom sparkled.

Why was I even thinking like this? I liked Flynn, but I don't think I could say I loved him. Yet. If ever. That was part of the reason I hadn't accepted his invitation to come to Scotland. If I went and I ended up falling in love with him, I would be in another hard situation. No matter the outcome, I would suffer.

Why couldn't things ever be easy?

My phone rang and I retrieved it from the bedroom.

It was Aleena.

"Please tell me you're not doing anything tonight," she said.

I laughed. "Why? Is Angus working?"

"Oh no. I've become one of those women, haven't I?"

"One of those women?"

"You know. The ones that abandon their friends when they fall in love."

I paused, astounded. "You're in love?"

"Oh, I don't know. Neither of us have said it yet, but you know what I mean. All your free time goes to the guy, and the friends end up on the back burner."

I recovered from my surprise. "Right. Don't worry. I can handle the back burner."

"Do you want to take front and center tonight? Yes, Angus is working, but I've missed you and I think we have some catching up to do. Let's go to dinner and see a movie."

"Yeah. That sounds fun."

We ate at Marigold's. We ordered salads, but that wasn't why we had picked Marigold's. I had been needing a piece of their chocolate chip cookie pie ever since Angus had told me they had eaten there on their first date.

"I could eat an entire pie," I said.

"No, you couldn't," Aleena said.

"I really think I could." I put another bite of pie and vanilla ice cream in my mouth.

Aleena giggled. "I know you couldn't eat a whole pie because last year, right after I broke up with that cute accountant, I bought a whole pie."

"You did?"

Aleena nodded. "I ate half of it in one night. It made me sick and I dreamed terrible dreams."

I laughed. "Okay, maybe just two pieces then."

Aleena waved down the waitress. "Could you bring us another piece of the pie and ice cream?"

"No, Aleena. I was just talking a big game."

"Yes, we do want one more. Don't worry," she said to me after the waitress had left. "We'll share it. I think I'll owe you whatever you want for the rest of your life."

"What are you talking about?"

"You know how there's that old legend that if you save someone's life, they're your servant forever? Or something like that. Well, I think there should be another one that if you're the match maker for a successful union, that couple should owe you dessert for life."

I laughed. "I think you might be on to something."

"Seriously, Charlotte, I can't even believe how wonderful Angus is. He's thoughtful, he's a hard worker, he's totally good-looking . . ." She took a bite of pie before she continued. "And he's an amazing kisser." She looked dreamy.

"He is?"

"Oh my. I can't even tell you."

"Good. Because I probably don't want to hear."

"All I can say is I'm glad you're delusional and actually think he's your brother, or you would have probably gone for him years ago."

I laughed. "I'm not delusional."

"Don't feel bad. I'm glad you're delusional. It's worked out great for me."

"You really like him, don't you?"

Aleena's face turned serious, and she leaned forward in her seat. "Charlotte, I'm pretty sure I'm falling in love with him."

"You are?" Angus is a great guy, so I'm not sure why her earnestness startled me.

She nodded. "Neither of us have said it, but I hope he's feeling the same way I am. Has he said anything to you? About me, I mean."

"He said you were amazing. And pretty. But I don't talk to Angus that much about who he's dating. He talks more to Will." Aleena looked a little disappointed that I didn't have more inside information. "But if the amount of time he spends with you is any indication, I would say you're in pretty good shape."

"He's so busy with his residency, but every time he has more than a day off, we go out."

"I'd say that must mean something."

Aleena smiled but didn't say anything.

I decided that over the last couple of months, Angus must have moved out of his apartment and moved into Aleena's brain. No matter what we talked about, she managed to work Angus into the conversation.

"How are your parents?"

"They're great. They really like Angus."

"Did your Dad's restaurant have any problem with those bad peanuts?"

"No, we were lucky. And anyway, Angus says they would only have made people sick if they already had a weak digestive system."

"Did you see how many points Curry scored last week?"

"Angus says Curry is the most underrated player in the NBA."

"I love that shade of yellow on you."

"Thanks. Angus says I look great in blue, so I try to wear other colors when I know I'm not going to see him."

Okay, that last one was a little exaggerated, but she did say Angus likes her in blue.

Aleena lit up when she talked about Angus, and I knew I had done a good thing setting them up. At least if I couldn't find the love of my life, maybe I could help them find theirs. I had made a good match for two of my favorite people. Maybe I had uncovered a new talent—matchmaking.

Chapter 14

I turned off the stereo in my car. What were the chances that I would hear "The One That Got Away" while I was driving to Fairfield for my birthday party? Okay, the chances were pretty good since I had put the song on a Kyle playlist, and that playlist was on shuffle. But still.

I had heard enough of the song to put me in a nostalgic mood and I thought about this drive to my parents' house the previous year. I had just met Kyle. In fact, a bouquet of flowers from him had ridden in the seat beside me. I had met Wyatt later that day when Angus brought her to our birthday party. I hadn't yet known about Kyle's political aspirations. I didn't know I would fall in love with him. I didn't know that one year later, I would barely be feeling like the stitches could be removed from my heart without it falling apart.

Angus would be here to celebrate again. That wasn't unusual. He had been to every birthday party I can remember. This year he was bringing Aleena. He had suggested to Will that he might come alone, but Will told me he had encouraged him to bring her. "She's one of Charlotte's closest friends. There's no reason she shouldn't come."

I should have been thrilled they were coming together, but after the awkwardness at Will's house a few weeks earlier, I wasn't quite as excited as I might have been. Hopefully there would be no kissing and strangeness to deal with today.

I arrived before anyone else so I could put together my contribution to the meal—a pasta salad. Mom had a vegetable tray almost finished, and Dad had the grill ready to go. We would begin barbecuing as soon as everyone arrived.

"Have you decided if you're going to Scotland?" Mom asked. I could tell it wasn't easy for her to broach the subject with a bright and happy voice, but since it was my birthday, she was giving it a valiant effort.

"I don't know, Mom. I keep going back and forth."

"And where are you today?"

"Right now I'm leaning against the idea. Flynn's such a nice guy, but I really don't need to complicate my life right now. The last year has been such a mess. I think I want to let things settle down before I make any big decisions."

Mom put the knife down on the butcher block where she had been cutting carrot sticks and stepped over to kiss my cheek. "With age comes wisdom."

I laughed. "Sometimes you're so dramatic." Mom smiled as she resumed her work. "And I'm not sure this last year has brought wisdom. I think it has just brought confusion."

"Things will work out in time. They always do."

Sunshine warmed the back deck, tempered every little while by a cool, gentle breeze that kept it from getting too hot. Flowers along the fence and in boxes and pots around the deck were blooming and scented the air. It was a lovely spring day for a family celebration.

I was excited for the food. After years of childhood favorites we'd long-ago outgrown, today we were trading in the chili dogs and macaroni and cheese for a barbecue. Mom had marinated chicken in a lemony glaze and Gina had brought her Paula Dean worthy potato salad. McKayla had made a chocolate cake with a cheesecake filling that she swore wasn't laced with illicit drugs, but I swear had to be just as addictive. I stopped myself at two pieces, but stashed a third in a Tupperware dish to take home with me.

"Next year, the only present I want from you is my own cake."

"That's easy. You're on," McKayla said. "Speaking of presents, are you guys ready to open them?"

I insisted Will open his first since he usually deferred to me. He was happy with his gifts. Dad and Mom gave him a band saw. "Now you won't have to borrow mine whenever you have a project."

"This is great, Dad. No more guilt for keeping it at our house for months at a time."

Connor and McKayla gave him one full day of labor. "We'll help you with any project you want. Maybe we can help you get that living room finished."

I gave Will a night at Blackbird Inn, a bed and breakfast in Napa. "And of course that comes with a built-in babysitter, you know."

Angus gave him a GoPole to go with his GoPro. "You just want to borrow this, right?" Will asked.

Angus laughed. "I promise I won't borrow it until you've had a chance to use it first."

Now it was my turn. I felt self-conscious, which surprised me. I've never felt uncomfortable with my family, but for some reason, today I did. Come to think of it, I felt uncomfortable most of the time now, like my life had shrunk two sizes and I didn't quite fit anymore.

The first gift I opened was a big, heavy box from Dad and Mom. It was a microwave. "Have you been talking to Mia?"

Mom shrugged. "She said yours has been broken since February."

"I was warming up some spaghetti and it started sparking and then the lights wouldn't stop flashing. I guess we should have replaced it a long time ago. Thank you. This is great."

Conner and McKayla gave me a pale pink floral skirt and a matching cardigan. "This is beautiful," I said, running my hand over the soft sweater.

"I knew you'd like it," McKayla said. "It's perfect for spring and summer."

Will and Gina gave me a day at the spa. "I should drive over there this afternoon and use it," I said.

"No. Go when you can get a full day," said Gina. "It includes everything. You've had a hard few months. We just thought it would be a nice break for you."

"And you don't have to worry about finding a date to go with you," Angus said. Why did everything he said to me anymore seem to be said with a dollop of sarcasm?

Gina looked embarrassed. "Would you have wanted a date to go with you? We just thought it would be more relaxing if you went alone."

"Of course not. This is perfect. No way would I want to take a date." I gave Angus a pointed look. "This is much better. And I won't have to scrounge up some poor guy and convince him to go with me."

Gina smiled. "Whew."

"I think that's a lovely gift," Mom said. She looked concerned about the tone of the conversation.

I looked at the last present—the one from Angus and Aleena—sitting on the table. It might as well have been an explosive devise ready to detonate as soon as I touched it. With tensions as palpable as they had been lately, I couldn't even imagine what Angus would give me. Then I remembered it was from Aleena, as well, and I breathed a little easier. She wouldn't allow him to give me a dead kitten.

I tore the paper off, and there in a mound of tissue were eight hand-painted knobs. "They're for that little dresser you refinished." I had told Aleena that someday I would replace the old knobs with something prettier and these were perfect.

"I love them. Thank you."

"There's something else in the bottom, too," Angus said.

"There is?" Aleena asked quietly and Angus nodded.

Under the rest of the tissue paper was a key ring with a whistle and pepper spray.

"That's a great gift," Dad said.

"Thanks, you guys," I said as I put it back in with the knobs. "No one better mess with me, right?"

"I figured you should have it before you go traipsing around the world with guys you barely know."

An awkward pall fell over the room as people looked around at each other. Only Angus didn't look around. He just looked at me.

What had gone wrong with us? Why had Angus become so mean and insulting? I felt like crying, but this wasn't just my birthday and I refused to ruin it for everyone else. But this had to stop. I couldn't stand it another second. I had to get to the bottom of it.

No one had said a word since Angus had spoken. I put the box at my feet and stood. "Could I talk to you for a minute?" I was looking directly at Angus and I managed to keep my voice steady and firm.

"Go ahead." He showed no signs of moving from his chair.

"No. Alone. In the house."

Finally, Angus glanced around the group. He shrugged. "Am I in trouble?" He was trying to make a joke, but no one laughed.

"We'll be right back," I said and walked ahead of him into the house.

I kept walking through the kitchen and into the living room, farther away from the party outside. I didn't want anyone to overhear our conversation or walk in on us. When I reached the fireplace, I turned around and faced Angus.

"What's going on, Angus?"

"What are you talking about?" Angus had a blank

look fixed on his face.

"Why are you constantly trying to pick a fight with me?"

"Don't exaggerate, Charlotte."

"And that. You only call me Charlotte when you're angry, and lately that's about all you call me."

Angus leaned back on the arm of the couch, facing me. "You've got to decide what you want, Charlotte. For years, you've been begging me to stop using nicknames. Now I do, and I'm in trouble for it. Make up your mind. What do you want? I can't keep up with you." His voice was like ice.

I shook my head, afraid I wouldn't be able to keep the tears at bay. "I don't know what I've done to make you so angry." A short laugh escaped from Angus. "Why don't you just tell me?"

"Maybe I'm just tired of picking up the pieces."

"The pieces?"

"The pieces of your broken heart. For years now you've made bad dating choices and every time it blows to pieces, you expect me to be there to rescue you."

I could hardly breathe. I had no idea he had resented me all this time. I had thought we were friends. I had thought he enjoyed getting together. If it was so awful, why had he called me when he'd had a breakup?

I swallowed over the marble that was lodged in my throat, threatening to suffocate me. "You should have said so. I didn't know you didn't want to go to therapy anymore. But don't worry, I won't call you again."

I hated that Angus was between me and the door and I would have to go around him to leave. I needed to be alone, to pull myself together. I needed him to stop looking at me.

I started toward the door, stepping to the side to get around him. I was almost past the spot where he sat when in one quick movement, he grabbed my wrist and pulled me into him.

And then his mouth was on mine and my mind was wiped of all thought. He pressed his lips against mine while his other hand came behind my neck and held me there firmly. The kiss was hot and frustrated and insistent. His hand let go of my wrist and moved to my back, pulling me closer.

And then the thoughts started coming, slowly, one at a time. *Angus is kissing me. This isn't a friendly hug. Holy smokes! ANGUS IS KISSING ME!*

And then the kiss softened, as if all the anger had been drained away and all that was left was gentleness, sweetness, and I didn't want to pull away. I put my arms around Angus's waist and moved my lips under his. *I'm kissing him back. Why am I kissing Angus?*

His mouth moved to the corner of mine and then his lips moved along my jaw, his warm breath by my ear as he let out a long sigh.

I didn't want to think about what it meant that Angus was kissing me. His lips traveled back to mine and I relaxed into his arms.

I felt weak and trembly. Aleena was right. Angus was an amazing kisser.

And then I froze.

Aleena.

I didn't want to—it was almost more effort than I

could summon—but I turned my face away and buried my forehead on his shoulder.

"Angus, what are you doing?" My voice cracked on the words.

I staggered back a step, but Angus caught my hand and held it in both of his. "What I should have done years ago."

I shook my head.

"Come on, Charles." His voice was gentle, pleading. His hands held mine, his thumbs brushing over my knuckles, his eyes never leaving my face. His voice was so quiet I had to strain to hear him over the percussion section in my chest and ears. "I've loved you forever."

The tears finally spilled over. "You've never said a word."

"I've wanted to, but you've never given me the chance."

"That's not true."

"Our timing has always been off. It's never felt like the right time."

I almost choked. "And this feels like the right time?"

Angus waited a moment before he spoke. "I wanted you to know. I know I've been pushing you to go to Scotland, but the truth is, I want you to stay here." His eyes met mine. "With me."

There was something so exposed and raw in Angus's expression, I felt like I was looking at an open wound. I wanted to pull him in my arms and ease his pain. But then I thought about Aleena sitting on the deck with my family, unaware of the betrayal that was happening just a few feet away.

"Angus." I shook my head and looked at the floor. "You shouldn't have done that."

"You kissed me back, Chuck."

"I shouldn't have."

"But you did. Don't tell me that doesn't mean something." I couldn't think about what it might mean. If I did, I might go crazy.

"What about Aleena? I thought you liked her."

Angus sighed. "I do like her. But she's not you. No one is you."

I met Angus's eyes, and the emotion I saw there scared me. "But she loves you. And she's my friend." I took another step back. "I can't be part of breaking her heart. I won't do that to her."

"You think I want to hurt her?" Angus's fingers stopped moving over my hand and then he let it go. "I didn't ask you to set us up, you know."

"You didn't stop me either."

"Because it's what you wanted."

"You should have told me." I couldn't stop the tears.

"I just did." With every word, his voice became more distant.

"It's too late, Angus. I don't want to hurt her."

Angus put his hands in his pockets and started to walk away. I reached for his arm to stop him. "Angus."

He turned to look at me, but I had no idea what to say. I wanted him to hug me and tell me we would always be friends but that wasn't fair. He had just handed me his heart, and I had shoved it back at him. What could I say after that?

"Chuck?" There was an ache in his voice that

shredded my insides. I let go of his arm and looked at his feet. "I had to try." His voice was full of pain, and he turned to go back outside.

I sat in the bathroom on the edge of the tub and cried. Mom knocked on the door to see if I was okay and I did my best to make my voice sound normal as I told her I was fine. I wasn't sure if I was disappointed or relieved when she walked away.

I wasn't even sure why I was crying. Was it because I had lost my best friend? Or was it more than that? I didn't dare examine the reasons too closely because of Aleena. What kind of friend would I be if I stepped in and destroyed what she had with Angus? I didn't even know how I felt about him, so there was no way I could justify taking him from her. Of course, I loved him. I had always loved him, but as a friend. As a confidant.

Suddenly, my entire relationship with Angus looked like nonsensical modern art with random pieces here and there that I couldn't explain.

I needed time and space to sort things out, to figure out my own mind and heart.

I splashed cold water on my face for a few minutes. I still looked a wreck, but nothing like I had ten minutes earlier.

There were several concerned glances cast my way when I rejoined the family on the deck. I must have looked surprised when I noticed Angus and Aleena's empty chairs because Will spoke up.

"They had to go. Angus said he had to get to the hospital."

McKayla looked concerned and mouthed the words, "Are you okay?"

I nodded.

I listened as the conversation shifted from sports to babies to ultrasounds. Everyone expressed shock that McKayla had thrown away the envelope containing the gender of their baby. "Technically Charlotte threw it away. If she hadn't been there, most of San Francisco would know what we're having." I pinned a smile to my face as the conversation evolved again and Connor asked Will when he wanted to redeem the day of home improvement labor.

"Maybe you can help him finish those beams. He's been working on them for weeks," Gina said.

"There were at least five coats of paint on them," Will said. "It's like an archaeological dig right there in my house. I wanted to finish the beams as a birthday present to myself, but they're still not done."

"There's always next year's birthday," Dad said.

"I'll help you finish them," said Connor.

"I've never given myself a birthday present before," I said. Suddenly everyone was looking at me. I think they weren't sure what had prompted me to join the conversation after remaining quiet for so long. "I think maybe this year I will."

McKayla leaned forward in her chair. "I hope it's something good."

"What do you have in mind?" Will asked.

"I think I'll go to Scotland."

Mom groaned, but Gina and McKayla exclaimed how exciting that would be.

This was the right thing to do. I needed to get away from here and where better to go than somewhere 4,851 miles away. It would be nice to see Flynn. He'd make me laugh. Maybe he could help me forget this ache in my stomach. If I wanted to, I could kiss him to my heart's content without feeling guilty about what I was doing to two of my best friends.

Oh Angus. Why did you have to ruin everything?

Chapter 15

"Hey, I'm sorry I missed you on your birthday." Flynn's smiling face filled my computer screen. "I even got up in the night to try to catch you when you got home from your party, but your computer must not have been on."

It had been on. I had heard it when I was washing my face, but it had stopped ringing before I could get there. I had stood there looking at the screen for a few minutes before I decided I wasn't ready to call him back. Sure, I'd just told my family I was going to Scotland, but I hadn't felt ready to tell Flynn. Now, two days had passed, and I still had reservations.

"I was pretty late getting home. Sorry you lost sleep for it."

"No worries. I was asleep again within minutes."

"That's good. Hey, I have news." I smiled like I was really excited.

"Let's hear it."

I took a gulp of air. "I'm coming to Scotland."

"You're not playin' with me, are ya?"

"Nope. I'm really coming. I talked to Jayne about it this morning. I just wanted to talk to you about when would be the best time. And a few other logistical things."

Flynn grinned. "Any time is the best time, so let's talk logistics."

"I need to know everything. Flight information. Hotels I can stay at. Exchange rate. All that stuff."

For the next few minutes, Flynn gave me the rundown on flights and hotels and sites I should see. His enthusiasm should have made me more excited about going, but the more he talked, the more I wondered if I was being unfair. I had no idea what his expectations would be or if he wanted anything to happen between us. I still didn't know if I did either.

"Charlotte?"

"Sorry. What?"

"Did you even hear what I just said?"

"About golfing?"

Flynn laughed. "That was a few minutes ago. I said if money is an issue, you can stay with my mum. Or maybe even Jessie. I could talk to them and see."

"Oh, I don't know about that. Your mom will probably hate that I'm coming. Jessie might too."

"Naw, they won't."

"Flynn?"

"Yes?"

"I don't know what I'm doing."

Flynn looked at me through the computer, and his face became gentle.

"I know what you're sayin' and you need to stop worrying yourself."

"I can't help it. Worrying seems to be what I do best. And sometimes I don't even know what I'm worrying about."

"Do ya want me ta tell ya?"

We both laughed. "Just because you've read my mind before doesn't mean you'll be able to again."

"True, but I'll bet I'm right."

"Fine. What's worrying me?"

"You want to come, but you still don't know if you should. You're worried I'll have the wrong idea about why you're coming. If you come, maybe we won't even like each other, and it might be weird. But if we do like each other, then what do we do?"

I shook my head. "Man, you're good."

Flynn lifted the corner of his mouth. "And you're a little afraid of my mum. You think she might not like you."

I laughed.

"How did I do?" he asked.

"Right on all counts."

"If it makes you feel better, Charlotte, I'm a little worried about all of it, too."

"Really?"

"Except for the part about my mum. I'm not afraid of her, and I know she likes me."

I smiled. "But the rest of it?"

"See, I want ya to come. And I think we'll be good friends. I don't think we need to worry about weird. So let's just take it that far and not think about what we'll do if lightning strikes us."

"You're right. We can do the friend thing."

Flynn nodded. "And if the other happens, we'll figure it out then."

"Thank you, Flynn. It's a little scary how you read my mind."

"Naw, it's a good thing. Especially since you're not good at sharing."

"I need to do better, don't I?"

"It would make my job easier."

"You're right. Okay. Let's make a deal that from this moment on, we'll tell each other exactly what we're thinking."

"And how we're feeling."

"Right."

"So what are you thinking, Charlotte?"

"That you're an amazing mind reader. And what are you feeling, Flynn?"

"Happy that you're coming to the Isle of Lewis."

"You're really going?"

"Please don't start. I'm giving you my whole Saturday afternoon, so the least you can do is not badger me."

Will and Connor had finally finished sanding down the beams, so when I had heard Gina was gone to her parents' and Will would be here staining the beams by himself, I had offered to come and help. Now we were both on ladders, our arms aching as we worked above our heads.

"I'm not badgering you. I'm just surprised you're

going. Mom said you told her you're not going and then suddenly you announced you were. You just have us all confused."

I didn't answer. I switched the brush to my other hand and shook my arm out.

"So what changed your mind?"

"A variety of things."

"And you're not going to tell me?"

"I don't want to bore you."

We worked in silence for a few minutes before Will looked at his watch. "I thought Angus might stop by to help for a little while."

"Really?" I didn't want to see Angus. If I had known there was a chance he would come by, I would have gone to a movie this afternoon or stayed home and done my laundry. Or volunteered to clean up elephant dung with my bare hands. Anything not to have to face him again. If Will saying his name made me blush at the thought of that kiss, how could I possibly look at him and keep my composure?

That kiss. I had replayed it over and over in my mind since that day. The frustration and pain behind it. The feel of his lips against mine. His breath on my neck. The fact that he'd loved me since forever. It was too much. This was Angus. I needed to put it out of my mind for good or I would never be able to act normal around him again.

"It's almost time for his hospital shift, so he's probably not coming."

I must have looked relieved because Will gave me a strange look. "Okay, Chuck. Spill it."

"Spill what?"

"What's going on with you and Angus?"

"Who says anything's going on?" I kept my eyes focused on the beam I was staining.

"You've both been acting weird lately."

"I haven't changed. He just gets upset with me all the time these days."

"Mmm hmm."

Will was leaning on the top rung of his ladder watching me. When he didn't look away, I gave him a cheesy grin. He smiled and resumed his work.

After a couple of minutes, Will spoke again. "Can I ask you a question?"

"Do I have a choice?"

"No."

"Fine. Ask away."

Will took a deep breath. "Have you ever thought about dating Angus?"

Stunned, I stared at him. "Why are you asking that?"

"I was just wondering."

"That idea didn't just pop into your head. Has Angus said something to you?"

Will shrugged. "I just know there was a time when he would have liked to date you."

"Why did he tell you and not me?"

"He's never told you?" I turned on the ladder so I was facing away from Will. He had always been pretty good at reading my face. "So he *has* told you."

"Sort of."

"But you weren't interested?"

I groaned. "I might have been. If the timing had been right."

"You two have always had bad timing."

"I'm not sure it would have been a good idea even if we had perfect timing."

"Why not?"

"Because it would probably ruin everything."

"What would it ruin?"

"Our friendship. The whole family thing. Right now he's like one of us. If we had dated and things hadn't worked out, he'd probably be embarrassed to come around. It would be uncomfortable."

"Yeah, Chuck. I don't know if you noticed, but our birthday party wasn't exactly calm and relaxed." I didn't answer. "Why do you think that is? What did you guys talk about when you went in the house?"

"I just asked him why he was being so mean and insulting lately."

"What did he say?"

"He didn't really have a good answer." I rested the brush on top of the can of stain. "I need a drink. You want me to get you something?"

"No, I'm fine. Don't duck out on me."

I climbed off the ladder. "Why would I do that?"

"You don't like this conversation?"

I laughed. "Don't worry. I'm not going anywhere."

I went to the kitchen and drank a glass of water. Will had known Angus was interested in dating me. How long had he known? Did others know? Was I the only one in the family who had been clueless?

I stood in the doorway. "Hey, Will, does everyone know?"

"Know what?"

I didn't even want to say the words. "That Angus wanted to date me."

"I don't know. Probably not. We've always talked to each other about girls."

I climbed back up the ladder, thinking. I had always thought Angus talked to me about girls and dating, too, but obviously he had left out one big, glaring detail.

"How long do you think this thing with your friend is going to last?" Will asked, interrupting my thoughts.

"Her name is Aleena, and there's no reason why it shouldn't last forever."

"Want to put any money on that?"

"Why? You don't think they're going to last?"

"Nope."

"Why not? She's amazing and beautiful and nice."

"Sounds like the last two or three women he's dated."

"Well, I hope it works. She really likes him." As the words came out of my mouth, I realized I wasn't sure if I meant them.

Will climbed off his ladder and moved it a few feet. "Then it probably hinges on how much he likes her."

"Has he talked to you about her?"

"Not much."

I felt sick inside, and I wasn't sure where to place the blame. Was it because Will thought my matchmaking attempt was going to fail? Or was it because I was afraid it would succeed? I loved Angus and Aleena. I just wasn't sure if I loved them together anymore.

Chapter 16

Travelers scurried around me as I checked the monitor at the Philadelphia International Airport. My flight would begin boarding at Gate B-9 in about two hours. That gave me time to find something to eat and to start the novel I had downloaded.

"Charlotte?" I turned to see who had said my name. "I thought that was you."

"Graham? What are you doing here?" Graham was Mia's on-again, off-again boyfriend of the past few years. I hadn't seen him in nearly a year.

"My brother and his wife live about an hour from here. I'm just headed home. Are you coming or going?"

"I'm just here for a couple of hours. I'm on my way to Scotland."

"Scotland. Wow. What's in Scotland?"

"A friend. Just going for a visit, seeing a new part of the world. Getting away for a couple of weeks."

"Sounds fun. I wish my vacation was just starting instead of ending." He hesitated before continuing. "How's Mia?" He fidgeted with the straps of his backpack.

"She's good." I lifted my messenger bag over my shoulder and stepped away from the monitor.

"Is she still working at Pratt?"

"Still there. She got a promotion in February."

"Good for her. Is she still running?"

"Not as much."

Graham looked at his watch. "I don't leave for more than an hour. Do you want to get something to eat?"

"Sure. I'm actually starving."

We walked until we found a kiosk that sold crepes. I ordered a turkey, cranberry and stuffing crepe and Graham chose one with strawberries and bananas. We sat down at a small, metal table under an awning that was trying and failing to look like a French street café.

"I'm surprised Mia's not running," Graham said. "We were going to do the San Francisco marathon. I thought she might still do it."

"I think when you left, she lost interest. I don't think she ever wanted to do it alone."

"Right."

We ate in silence for a minute.

"I know you don't really like me," Graham started.

I shook my head. "That's not—" Graham held up his hand to stop me.

"Let me say this, Charlotte. I don't blame you. I wouldn't like me either. But I want you to know I've never left because of another girl."

I put down my fork and looked at Graham. I was surprised to see how emotional he appeared.

"Listen, Graham. I don't dislike you. I never have. But I love Mia, and I hate seeing her yanked around and hurt."

"I hate it too."

"But you keep doing it to her."

Graham lowered his head. "I know. I've tried to stay away this time. I don't want to hurt her anymore. I love her."

"Then what's the problem?"

Graham took a deep breath and let it out through his teeth. "I just don't want to make a mistake. I've watched my parents get married over and over and over, and I don't want that to be me."

"Then don't be like them." I took a bite of my crepe.

Graham let out a short, derisive laugh. "It's not that simple."

I could tell Graham was upset, and I felt bad for him, but he was looking at things all wrong. If he loved Mia, he needed to stop hurting her. And himself. The longer we sat there, the more frustrated I became.

"Yes it is, Graham." My voice came out more determined than I had meant for it to. In fact, it probably sounded angry because Graham looked stunned. "It's as easy or as hard as you decide to make it. Mia's great. She's one of the easiest people in the world to get along with. In fact, the only time we've really disagreed has been when she wanted to keep giving you chances, and I thought she should move on. If you love each other, then have a little faith in each other. I know Mia has faith in you. More than I think you deserve."

Graham barely nodded, but it was enough to let me know he was listening. "Does your brother have the same parents as you?" Graham's nod became a little bigger, and

I made my voice a little softer. "And he's married."

"I know. I watched them this trip with their little boy, and I felt like such a failure."

"So don't fail. Find someone to love and then take a leap of faith."

Graham looked shell-shocked. "Is Mia . . ." His voice trailed off, and then he tried again. "Is Mia involved with someone?"

"No. She's dated a few people, but none of them have stuck." Graham looked relieved. "But Graham, please don't show up on our doorstep again unless you're ready to commit to her. You've hurt her enough."

"I know."

"Sorry to be hard on you, but—"

"Charlotte, you don't have to explain. I know."

We ate in silence for several minutes, and then Graham leaned back in his chair, his thoughts far away. Probably in San Francisco.

"Listen," I said, scooting to the edge of my chair. "I'm going to head over to my gate."

Graham pulled himself out of his thoughts and stood up. "Sure. Thanks, Charlotte. It was good to see you."

"You too. I'm not going to tell Mia I saw you." There was no way I wanted to get her hopes up when Graham was so unpredictable.

"I understand. Have a good trip."

I was a couple of gates away when I glanced back at Graham. He was sitting back down, his head resting in his hand.

It had been a month since I had told Flynn I was coming. If I'd had a passport, I would have booked a flight and left the night of my birthday. Even though I paid for an expedited passport, it had still taken more than three weeks.

It was good I hadn't been able to leave immediately. Waiting a month made me feel better about the trip. It gave me time to convince myself that I wasn't running away from something. And it had given Flynn and me time to come to a clear understanding. As I boarded my plane, I realized I was excited to see him. I was thrilled to see Scotland. I had poured over travel websites and had decided this was just what I needed. I would spend two days in Glasgow before flying to Stornoway. Flynn had offered to meet me in Glasgow and be my tour guide, but I wanted to do it alone. There would be plenty of time for him to be a guide once I arrived on the Isle of Lewis.

I managed to get a few hours of sleep on the plane, and I arrived in Glasgow early in the morning. A short cab ride later, I was at The Hotel Glasgow. It was too early to check in so the concierge took care of my luggage while I waited in the lobby to meet my tour.

I laughed to myself as my fellow travelers gathered together. I would have to tell McKayla she had been right. She had teased me when I had shown her the tour I was taking.

"You're going to be traveling with a bunch of retirees," she had said. "You'll probably be the only one under sixty."

The only thing she had been wrong about is the number of us who weren't retired. There were three of us—me, a blonde in her thirties who looked to be the young trophy wife of an elderly man who looked like Larry King but with thicker glasses, and her son, a boy of about twelve. At first I had thought she was the old man's daughter, but that misconception was quickly erased when they kissed. It was a messy, gag-inducing kiss that made me quickly look away. The poor boy looked like he wanted to make a run for the door.

I had never traveled by myself, and I felt a surge of pride at my independence. Mom and Dad hadn't been thrilled about it. That's when I had agreed to book real tours instead of renting a car and setting off by myself. It was a reasonable compromise, and I'd had fun picking the tours I would take.

"Welcome to Highland Tours," said a pretty girl with strawberry blonde hair, pale green eyes, and a plaid bowtie. "If you'll follow me to the coach, we'll be on our way."

I didn't care where I sat as long as I didn't have a view of Mr. King and his arm candy. I dropped into the first available seat and scooted over to the window. I was sliding my purse under my seat when a pair of purple running shoes stopped in the aisle beside me.

"Is someone joining you?" I didn't have to look up very far to see the diminutive woman who spoke. I could tell by her accent that she was American, probably from somewhere in the east. Her gray hair was styled in a short, messy pixie cut that would have made a Hollywood celebrity proud. She wore a purple, velour track suit, her nails were painted purple and the lenses of her glasses had a purple tint.

"Nope. It's just me."

"Do you mind?" She pointed at the spot next to me.

"Not at all."

"Thank you." She settled into the seat, her feet a couple of inches off the floor. She really was tiny.

She turned to me once she had stowed her lavender bag under the seat and put out her hand. "I'm Lucy."

"I'm Charlotte," I said, shaking her hand.

"Nice to meet you, Charlotte." She lowered her glasses and peered at me closely. "I'm traveling alone because my Frank died last year. What's your excuse?"

I couldn't help but laugh. "Do I need an excuse?"

"I suppose not. You kids do all kinds of things we'd have been afraid of when I was your age."

"You don't seem afraid right now."

She patted my arm with her violet-nailed hand. "Don't be fooled. I'm plenty afraid. I'm just blustering my way through the fear." She turned in her seat and craned her neck to see the other passengers. "Frank made me promise I would come do this, so here I am."

"He made you promise to travel?"

"Not just anywhere. Here. To Scotland. We talked about this trip for years—we both have ancestors from here—but then Frank up and died two months before he was supposed to retire."

"I'm sorry."

"Me too. But a promise is a promise, so here I am."

"Ladies and gentlemen. Welcome to our tour today. My name is Margaret, and I'm happy to be sharing our lovely country with you. Our first stop will be Inveraray Castle. This beautiful castle is the ancestral home of the

Duke of Argyll, the chief of the Clan Campbell. To get to Inveraray, we'll be driving through Loch Lomond National Park, but don't worry when we don't stop. We'll make a few stops in the park on our way back. After we tour the castle, we'll eat lunch at the King George Pub. It's a cloudy day, but with a little luck, we'll all stay dry. To your left is The University of Glasgow. It boasts one of the oldest and largest university libraries in all of Europe, with more than two and a half million books and journals."

It was more than an hour from Glasgow to the castle. Many of the buildings we passed had been there for hundreds of years. It was crazy to think that some of these homes had been built before settlers had even discovered gold in California. Even America's oldest places were new when you compared them to Scotland.

"When we arrive at the castle, you're welcome to take the formal tour or you can wander the castle and grounds on your own. We would just ask that ya not go behind any of the roped off areas. Be back on the bus at 1:00 or we'll have to leave ya, and you'll miss out on lunch at the King George Pub."

"Are you taking the tour?" Lucy asked as we exited the bus.

"I think I'm going to take off on my own," I said.

"Good for you." Lucy gave an energetic fist pump. "If I don't run into you in the castle, I'll see you back on the bus."

The sky was overcast, the air humid but warmer than I had expected after riding in the air-conditioned coach. My feet crunched in the tiny gravel that covered the narrow road that led to the castle.

The Inveraray Castle sat on a rise overlooking the River Aray. Behind the castle, rolling, tree-covered hills disappeared into the low-lying clouds. The gray stone structure was surrounded by gardens bursting with colorful flowers.

The interior of the castle was grand and ornate and filled with Scottish history. The crest of the Campbell Clan could be seen in artwork throughout the castle and their signature plaid was even used on one of the large canopy beds.

While the castle was certainly beautiful, there was something about the grounds that called to me. I wandered through the flowering gardens down a path bordered by sculpted shrubs that opened onto a sloping lawn so green, it almost looked artificial. Beyond the lawn was the Aray River and a beautiful stone bridge. I started across the grass.

Even though clouds covered the sun, it didn't take long before the exertion of my walk made me warm. I took off my jacket and tied it around my waist. I liked the smell in the air—grassy and earthy.

A couple of tourists smiled and greeted me as they walked back to the castle. By the time I reached the water's edge, there were only a couple of other people by the river.

I touched the ground to see if it was damp and finding it dry, I sat down. The only sound was the river. It was so quiet and peaceful. I looked back at the castle. It was certainly beautiful and impressive, but if I lived here, I would want a pretty stone cottage down here by the water.

I sat cross-legged for quite a while, thinking about

my life in San Francisco. How had things gone so wrong? A year ago my life had been nearly perfect—a great job, a handsome boyfriend, and Angus, my best friend. I still had the job, but the boyfriend was gone and Angus seemed completely lost to me, which meant Aleena was probably leaving my life, as well. If they fell in love and married, how could I ever be around them knowing what had happened and what Angus had said. I would probably still see them on occasion, but it wouldn't be comfortable or easy.

My mind wandered for the thousandth time to The Kiss. That's what I called it now. With capital letters. Even though Angus wasn't my first kiss, his was the only one that regularly crept into my mind. If I heard someone say the word "kiss," Angus's kiss in my parents' living room is the one I thought of. It could have been a perfect kiss if it hadn't been a betrayal of Aleena, and if it hadn't robbed me of Angus's friendship, and if I hadn't been too stunned to know what was happening. I sighed. It had felt like a perfect kiss in spite of all that. At least for a moment.

Now that I wasn't walking, the cool air started to feel chilly. Goose bumps rose on my arms and I shivered. I could have put my jacket back on but I liked the slightly unpleasant feeling. It distracted me from The Kiss and seemed to anchor me in Scotland. I was here, far away from my years of heartache and problems and disappointments. Now if only I could avoid creating more. I looked at my cell phone and decided I had time to walk over the bridge.

It had been a lovely day. Lunch at the King George Pub had been fun. Margaret had told us the décor hadn't changed in a couple of centuries. We had sat at a wooden table so old that time and the hands of the many people who had eaten there had polished it as smooth as glass. She said the pale, velvet curtains had once been a deep maroon. We ate chicken pies with the flakiest crust I had ever eaten.

We stopped a few times to admire the sites in Loch Lomond National Park as we returned to Glasgow. I was eager to get some dinner to eat in my room and then fall into bed.

We were almost to the hotel when Lucy put her hand on my arm. "If you don't have plans for dinner, Charlotte, I would love for you to join me. I really hate eating alone. I can just imagine everyone watching me and feeling sorry for me."

I watched the quiet dinner I had been looking forward to disappear. How could I turn down this sweet woman who was fulfilling a promise to her husband? "That would be nice. I'd planned on eating at the restaurant in our hotel. Does that sound okay?"

"I ate there last night and it was underwhelming. I asked Ian, the concierge, where he would suggest, and he recommended City Merchant. He says they have the best seafood in town. Oh, I don't know if you like seafood."

"I love seafood."

"Oh good. I thought maybe we could go there, if you're game."

I smiled. "That sounds great."

We parted ways at the hotel to change for dinner. I

unlocked the door and saw my room for the first time. It was small, but comfortable and surprisingly modern, considering the age of the hotel. My bags were waiting neatly in front of the tiny dresser in the corner. I changed into a gray skirt and a red sweater, freshened up my makeup and brushed my teeth. Since I had fifteen minutes to spare before I was to meet Lucy in the lobby, I sent a quick email telling my family I had arrived safely, stretched out on the bed, and dialed Flynn's number.

That was a mistake. Not the calling Flynn part. The bed part. The pillows were fluffy and crisp, the bed soft and comfortable.

"Hullo." Flynn sounded close. I knew it was crazy to think it was because I was less than three hundred miles away from Stornoway. He probably didn't sound any different than if I had talked to him on a phone at home instead of Skyping.

"Hi Flynn. I'm in your country."

"Brilliant. And how do ya like it?"

"Today was wonderful. I went to Inveraray Castle and The King George Pub and I'm now getting ready to go to City Merchant with a cute, little purple woman I met on my tour."

"You met one of our famous purple people?"

I laughed. "Actually, she is one of our famous purple people. She's American."

"And I thought we had the corner on purple people."

"Right now I'm wishing she hadn't invited me. I'm so tired and this bed is so comfortable."

"Hopefully your friend won't want to go hit the clubs after dinner."

"I think I'm safe. She's got to be in her sixties, at least."

"A sixty year old with purple hair?"

"Her hair's not purple, but just about everything else is. She has purple glasses and shoes and clothes. Even her fingernails are painted purple."

"Your mission tonight is to find out why she likes purple so much. You can fill me in tomorrow."

"Ooh, a mission. I'll see what I can find out."

"I'm glad you've come, Charlotte."

"Me too."

"We're going to have a grand time, and you're going to feel like a new person." Why was it so easy for Flynn to read me?

"Why do you think I need to feel like a new person? What's wrong with the old person?" I was trying to tease, but as soon as the words were out, I knew they had come across more needy and desperate and distraught than I had meant. My ability to flirt and tease seemed to have died. Or at least it was hanging by a thread.

"There's nothing at all wrong with the old Charlotte. Except that she needs this vacation."

I sighed. "And a good night's sleep." I looked at the clock beside the bed. "It looks like I'd better go meet Lucy."

"Enjoy your dinner. I'll see you tomorrow night."

Tomorrow night. A few months ago, I hadn't met Flynn, and the thought of traveling to Scotland hadn't even entered my mind. Now here I was, traveling alone, seeing new places and having new experiences. Maybe this would be where I would finally find peace and happiness and healing.

Chapter 17

I didn't immediately see Lucy when I stepped out of the elevator. She wasn't sitting on one of the overstuffed sofas near the fireplace or standing by the front doors. And then something purple caught my eye. Lucy stood in the far corner of the lobby talking to the concierge. She had changed from her purple track suit to a flowing purple dress. An ivory scarf with purple flowers was tied like a headband around her hair, the scarf ends trailing down her back. She looked elegant and stylish.

"Ian says the restaurant is about six blocks away. I thought maybe we could walk and then take a cab back, since it will be dark when we finish dinner. Unless you're too tired. If you'd prefer, we can take a cab both ways."

"I don't mind walking." If Lucy could walk the six blocks after a long day, so could I.

"Thank you, Ian." Lucy said. "You've been a dear."

"Have a good evening, ma'am. Miss." He nodded toward me.

The sunshine must have been saving its energy all day so it could put on a show this evening. It danced through trees and sparkled against windows. In some places it seemed to be doing the limbo as it slanted under fences and fit into impossible corners. It painted the sidewalk with our long, abstract shadows and dazzled us with colorful pink and purple clouds before it finally bowed its way off the stage.

"I wish Frank could have seen this. He always wanted to come to Glasgow. His mother was born here and lived here until she married an American that was stationed here during the war. I had a cab take me by the house she lived in yesterday. Nothing too exciting, but when you know his mother lived there, it makes it special."

"I'm sure he would be glad to know you came to see it."

"Yes, he would have. My great-grandmother lived in Wallyford, just outside Edinburgh, so I'm heading there tomorrow."

"How did your husband die?"

"He died during open heart surgery. But he would have died without it, too, so it was a chance we had to take."

"I'm sorry."

"I miss him. He was a good man."

City Merchant had a pretty, teal-blue façade. Stained glass windows that featured bright yellow fish swimming through the ocean cast colorful spots on the sidewalk.

The hostess seated us at a little table by the front window where we could watch the people on the street. I realized they could see us as well when a man winked at me and a little girl waved. Lucy waved and smiled and seemed comfortable being on display.

"You look nice tonight. I love your scarf," I said.

Lucy patted the scarf lightly. "Thank you. Frank always liked it when I dressed up, so I'm trying to look nice. Just in case he's watching me take this trip." She blew a kiss toward heaven.

"You really like purple, don't you?"

She leaned across the table like she was sharing a secret, and I knew I might be about to succeed at my mission. "Just after Frank and I were married, he gave me a purple dress. It was so purple it almost hurt your eyes, and I couldn't imagine wearing so much purple at once, but I hugged him and thanked him anyway. Then he said, 'You look so beautiful when you wear your purple sweater, I knew I had to get this for you when I saw it.' And you know what, he was right. I always got compliments when I wore that sweater, and I got compliments when I wore that dress. Every time Frank bought me clothes, he bought purple, and pretty soon I started to choose that color. Now, more than forty years later, that's about all I have. My grandkids keep their grandmothers straight by calling me the purple grandma."

I smiled. "Well, he did you a favor then because it suits you."

We both ordered the Hebridean salmon special and sat back to wait for our food. Outside, old-fashioned streetlamps sputtered several times and finally stayed lit. The street looked foreign and romantic.

"I've been talking Frank, Frank, Frank ever since I met you. Tell me about you, Charlotte. What are you doing here in Scotland alone?"

"I'm just here in Glasgow until tomorrow night, and then I'll be flying to the Isle of Lewis."

"Where's that?"

"It's part of Scotland. It's an island off the west coast."

"Sounds wild and remote."

"I've never been there. A friend of mine lives there."

"How nice. How did you meet her?"

I took a sip of water. "It's a he." I told Lucy about Flynn and how we met.

"What a romantic story. That'll be a fun one to tell your children and grandchildren."

I laughed. "We're just friends."

"Oh, Charlotte, take it from a wise old woman. Friends make the best husbands."

"Did you and Frank start out as friends?"

"No. We fell madly in love almost the moment we met. Couldn't keep our hands off each other. Frank laid a kiss on me our first date that would have killed me if I hadn't had a strong heart." I cringed a little at that, knowing her husband had died during open heart surgery, but Lucy didn't seem to notice. "We started out with fire and passion, but we were the lucky ones."

"What do you mean?"

"Let me tell you about Frank and his two brothers." Lucy shifted excitedly in her seat as she prepared to tell her story. "There were three boys in Frank's family—Frank, Jimmy, and Paul. Frank fell madly in love with me, and we got married not quite a year later. We were lucky though, because behind all that lusty infatuation were two people who had a lot in common. We didn't know it at the time, but we liked the same movies and we both enjoyed playing games and laughed at the same kinds of jokes. Once we had been married a while, we settled into a real comfortable marriage. We could talk easily, and we could tell what the other one needed. If I'd had a hard day, Frank didn't even need to ask. He could tell when he walked in the door and he knew exactly what to do. Sometimes he'd offer to take the kids to the park or he would ask if I wanted him to go get some groceries. And I could tell the same about him. If he'd had a hard week at work, I would tell him he should call his brothers and go golfing Saturday morning or I would make him his favorite carrot cake. We became best friends."

"It sounds like you had a perfect marriage," I said.

"Oh my, no. There's no such thing as a perfect marriage. But if you're friends, you can get through all the imperfect stuff together. Paul and his wife, Ivy, started out different than us, but ended up the same. Their families were friends before Paul or Ivy were even born. They played in diapers together and went to the same school. Even went to the same college. One day Ivy realized she wanted to marry Paul. So she told him. Paul thought she was crazy, and he told her so. Said he was waiting for sparks and fireworks. She said, 'you want sparks and fireworks? Here ya go.' And she kissed him. He told her he didn't feel a thing and it about broke Ivy's heart. But that kiss did its job. Paul couldn't stop thinking about it, and after a few weeks, he called Ivy and invited her to dinner. And that was that. They got married two months later."

"What about Jimmy?"

Lucy shook her head. "Now that's a sad story. Jimmy

had a hard time because he was always looking for the passion. He always fell in love at first sight—which probably isn't love, if you know what I mean." She said that quietly, behind her hand. "Frank kept telling him he needed to get to know a girl first but Jimmy reminded him about us. Frank told him we were the lucky ones that fell hard and then became good friends but he wasn't really interested. He said, 'I've got plenty of buddies. I don't need a girl to be my friend.'"

"So what happened to him?"

Lucy shook her head. "He had many, many girlfriends, but they never lasted. He got married once, but after the sparks quit flying, they couldn't stand each other. They divorced after about four years of fighting. He swore off marriage and said he wasn't cut out for it, but we always thought it would have been different if he would have married someone he liked."

"How sad for him."

"Yes, it was. He never had a family. He died the year before Frank did."

"How are Paul and Ivy?"

Lucy reached into her bag and pulled out a little book. She showed me pictures of her daughter and son and of Paul and Ivy and their five children. She put the little book away when our food arrived.

As much as Lucy liked to talk, I think she liked to eat even more. Conversation was sporadic while we ate as she focused on her meal.

I was glad. It gave me a chance to think, and I was surprised at where my thoughts led. The conversation about falling in love with a friend had been in response to my assertion that Flynn and I were just friends. But now it wasn't Flynn I was thinking about. It was Angus.

I thought of Angus helping me study so I could pass my math classes. We had helped each other through years of dating and breakups and he was right. He had always been there to pick up the pieces when things went wrong. And I had been there for him. I had edited papers for him and taken him dinner when he was studying for his medical school entrance exams. I had helped him with an elaborate plan to ask a girl to prom our senior year. We'd had an English class together our junior year so we had read *The Grapes of Wrath* and *Pride and Prejudice* aloud together, because I hadn't wanted to read *The Grapes of Wrath,* and he hadn't wanted to read *Pride and Prejudice.*

We had shared so much together. He really was my best friend.

I thought about Ivy kissing Paul. That's exactly what Angus had done. The difference was that Paul had thought about it and then asked Ivy out. I had thought about it—obsessed about it even—but I had completely ignored Angus. I hadn't seen him or said one word to him since that night.

All I had felt was anger. I was upset with him for kissing me. I didn't want to feel what I had felt during that kiss. I was angry at him for putting me in a position where I might hurt Aleena. I was furious at him for letting me set him up with her. If he wasn't interested in being set up, he should have told me. There were a lot of things he should have told me. Maybe things would have been different if he had been honest.

Everything was such a mess. I didn't want to think

about it anymore. I wanted to quit feeling angry and ashamed and frustrated and disappointed. I wanted to be happy again.

"Thinking about that 'friend' you're about to see?" Lucy was a smart woman with a lot of wisdom, but she couldn't read my mind the way Flynn did.

"I guess so," I lied. "I'm looking forward to tomorrow night." That part wasn't a lie.

I hugged Lucy goodbye in the lobby. "Enjoy the rest of your trip," I said.

"Enjoy the rest of your life, young lady." She hugged me tightly and then reached up and patted my cheek. "Thank you for sharing the day with me."

Even though I was exhausted, sleep didn't come easily. Too much was happening in my head. It was well after midnight before my tired body finally overcame my mind, and I drifted off into a restless sleep.

Chapter 18

*L*ights grew closer as the small plane descended. That must be Stornoway. Judging by the number of lights, it was a smaller town than I had realized. The flight from Glasgow had been short—only about an hour long. I was glad because it had been the most turbulent hour I had ever spent on a plane. The pilot said it was because of a storm front but I didn't really care what caused it. I just wanted to land safely.

There were only nine passengers on the flight, and based on little conversations I overheard, only three of us were tourists. The couple sitting two rows behind me were on their way to see the Arnol Blackhouse, but everyone else, it seemed, was going home. The man sitting across the aisle knew the crew by their first names.

"Tell Luke to hold 'er steady up there. He's not scrambling eggs back here."

"Luke and I aren't talkin'. He called me a dunderhead, so if ya have somethin' to say to Luke, you'll have to tell him yourself. What are ya flying home on a Tuesday for, anyway?"

"Meetings got cancelled for the rest of the week."

The plane taxied to a stop, and my nerves started buzzing like a light bulb that can't decide if it's ready to burn out or not. It was easy to talk to Flynn through the computer, but what if we had nothing to say in person?

I took a deep breath and gathered my things.

We exited the plane down a portable staircase onto the asphalt. No ramps and tunnels that led directly into the airport here. A wall of floor to ceiling windows forty feet away spilled light into the dark and I started toward the door where I could see a few people gathered.

I saw Flynn as soon as I walked through the door. He wore a navy blue shirt and a khaki barn jacket. His hair was a little messy, like he had been standing in the wind. I hardly had time to wonder if I was supposed to wave or shake his hand or hug him before he had wrapped me in a welcoming hug that felt as good as a warm bowl of soup.

"Welcome to Stornoway, Charlotte."

A few minutes later, my bags were stowed in the back seat of Flynn's little car and we were leaving the airport.

"You weren't lying when you said you drove a little car, too."

"What? You thought I was lying?"

I shrugged. "I thought maybe you were just trying to make me feel better about squishing you in my little car."

"You should always believe me. How was your day?"

I told Flynn about my tour of Glasgow. "I'm glad ya saw the People's Palace. We went on a field trip there when I was in school."

"You flew to Glasgow for a field trip?"

"Naw, we took the ferry. Were ya lonely? I could have

come with you today."

"I was fine. It was nice to be able to wander by myself and not have to worry about keeping a conversation going. It was a good day."

"Already insulting my conversation skills?"

"I didn't mean that. Sorry."

"Charlotte, I'm just teasin' ya. Tell me what you learned about the purple lady last night."

"Her husband liked her in purple so that's what she always wore. Now she hardly owns anything else."

"Ah, that's nice."

"She was a very sweet lady. Wise too. I'm glad I joined her."

Flynn drove me to the Thorlee Guest House. We gathered my bags, and after I had checked in, we walked to the small, second story room.

Flynn sat down in a straight-backed chair at a tiny table and I sat on the bed.

"Charlotte, I've got a proposition for ya, and I don't want you to say no without thinking about it. In fact, I don't want ya to say no at all, but especially not before you've slept on it."

"This sounds serious."

Flynn drummed his fingers on the table before he started. "You're here for nine nights. This room is more than a hundred pounds per night, so all together that's going to cost you over a thousand pounds. That's too much for a trip to see me."

I raised an eyebrow. "You think I'm here to see you?"

Flynn laughed. "I want ya to stay at my place. I've already talked to Mum, and I'm staying with her the whole time you're here, so if ya don't stay in my house, it'll sit there empty and lonely."

"Flynn, I don't want to kick you out of your house."

"You're not. This will save you money, you'll have your own place and I'll be right next door if you decide you want to go exploring in the middle of the night. There's still a bed in my old room at Mum's, and my old posters of the Dundee United soccer team on the walls. I'm looking forward to it. I'll fall asleep looking at those posters and dreamin' I was on the team."

"But I've paid for this."

"I've already talked to Carl and explained the situation. He'll refund your money for the rest of your trip. You can stay here tonight so you can experience the old Scottish inn and then tomorrow we'll move ya to my place."

"Are you sure?"

"Positive."

"Thank you. That sounds great." The thought of saving almost two thousand dollars was comforting. I had drained a big chunk of my savings for this trip, so putting some of it back would be a relief.

"I'm opening the store tomorrow. Jessie'll get there about eleven, so I'll come pick you up then."

"Thanks, Flynn."

Flynn stood and pulled me up off the bed and into his arms. He smelled like laundry soap and sawdust and wind. "If you want to tell me why you decided to come, I'm happy to listen."

"What do you mean?" I said into his shoulder, glad he couldn't see my face.

"I don't think it was my charm that made you change your mind, so I think something must have happened. If you ever want to talk about it, we can."

I nodded into his shirt, and he ran his hand down the length of my hair before he stepped back. "I'll stop and tell Carl you're checking out tomorrow. See you in the morning."

I stood in the doorway until Flynn turned the corner, then I closed and locked the door.

"Stornoway looks larger today," I said when we left the inn.

"There are more than nine thousand people who live in Stornoway."

"That many, huh?" I smiled and elbowed him.

"That's not many compared to San Francisco, but we've got everything we need. Right over there is the primary school where Bruce and I went." I looked at the small school and tried to imagine a little Flynn and Bruce learning their letters and playing games at recess.

Every street held a memory for Flynn and he shared them in a funny way. He was a good storyteller and I enjoyed listening to him. "See that butcher shop? One year I decided I was tired of working in the hardware store, so I asked Mr. Potter if I could work for him. He needed someone to grind the meat and fill the sausages. I wanted to quit after the first day. My hands were slimy and I smelled terrible. But Dad said I'd wanted the change so now I had to give Mr. Potter a fair effort. He made me work there six months before I could quit. I think he did that on purpose so when I came back to the hardware store, I'd be thankful to work there. Any time I start to get sick of stocking shelves and ordering nails, I remember grinding meat and stuffing sausages.

"Smart dad."

"Aye. And here we are. Macgruger Hardware."

The store sat between a PharmX, a corner pharmacy, and a bookstore called Books. The window display had a ladder with an open tool box overflowing with tools sitting beside it. Painted on the window was a list of sale items: Hoses – 20% off, Assorted Garden Tools – Buy one get one ½ off, Weed killer – 15% off. Golf balls – Buy one get one free.

"Golf balls?" I asked.

Flynn shrugged. "We've still got Dad's little golf corner."

The bell above the door rang as we walked inside.

"Flynn, can you help me?" a woman asked.

"Hi, Doreen. What do you need?"

"Daniel asked me to come pick up some furnace filters, but I have no idea what kind to get."

"I can show you what he always buys," Flynn said. "I'll be right back," he said to me and walked down an aisle with Doreen.

"Can I help you find something?" asked a woman's voice. I turned around and recognized Jessie. She was shorter than I had thought. And prettier. She smiled. "Oh, you're not a customer. You're Charlotte."

"And you're Jessie, right?"

"Right. It's great to meet you. What's Flynn doing

196

leavin' ya stranded like this?"

I pointed the direction Flynn had gone. "He went to help a customer with a filter or something."

"Of course. How are ya liking Scotland?"

"It's beautiful. I really liked Glasgow."

"I love Glasgow. It's so busy and loud. But after a few days there, I like to come back to Stornoway."

"Jessie, could you ring her up?" Flynn asked. Doreen now stood at the cash register with her furnace filters.

Jessie helped the customer while Flynn gave me a tour of the store. It was larger than I had thought it would be. There were about a dozen aisles of merchandise. "Back here's the yard where we keep lumber and some of the bigger things." The yard wasn't really a yard. It wasn't even outside. It was just a large room that felt like a warehouse with a garage door at the back. "And here's the golf corner."

I had to laugh. It wasn't big, but the section was carpeted with artificial grass and even had a tiny putting green. The two walls were lined with golf equipment—clubs, bags, and balls. It felt very out of place among all the hardware and building supplies.

"Jessie, we're going out to the Crawford's. Mom'll be here soon, so you can go to lunch."

"Brilliant." I smiled. It reminded me of Flynn. "It was nice to meet you, Charlotte."

"I hope I'll see you again," I said.

"Oh, ya will for sure. Flynn's bringing ya to the fire, I hope."

I looked at Flynn. "I hadn't mentioned it yet, but we'll probably be there."

The Crawfords lived several miles outside of town. We hadn't met a single car since just outside of Stornoway. "This road doesn't look wide enough for two cars," I said.

"It is. It's a tight fit, but it works."

A short time later, we passed a small truck loaded with hay. Each car had a wheel on the tiny shoulder of the road, but we made it.

The houses grew farther and farther apart until it had been a mile since we had passed the last one. Before we reached the top of a hill, the road curved around to the other side and I caught my breath. Nestled against the hill was a clean, white house. It wasn't large or pretentious, but the view would have made it a million dollar home in San Francisco. Lush, green hills sloped away to the sea. Little pockets of the sea snaked their way inland, creating a kaleidoscope of greens and blues unlike anything I had ever seen before.

"The colors," I said, almost speechless.

"The water's not always blue like that. When it's cloudy, it's gray."

"I thought you were exaggerating about heaven, but you weren't." Just beyond the Crawford's white house was the smaller, unfinished guesthouse. "This is what you're building?"

"Come on. I'll show you."

It wasn't large, just a great room and two small bedrooms. The exterior walls were up, but the inside was just framed, so you could see from one side of the house to the other.

"The outside will be white siding, like the main house. See that stone?" Flynn pointed outside at a pile of flat, gray rocks. "I'll be using those for the fireplace. Right here."

I walked to the front of the room and looked out the large window. There wasn't another sign of human life—no houses, no roads, no people. Just grasses blowing in the breeze and water as far as you could see. "This might be the most beautiful place I've ever seen."

Flynn came up behind me and wrapped his arms around my shoulders. "It can be pretty brutal out here during the winter, but the summer makes up for it."

I didn't want to leave this place. I wanted to walk until I reached the water. I wanted to see the houses up here in the side of the hill from that farthest finger of land. I'd have probably started down the hill if Flynn hadn't begun describing more of the plans he had to finish the house.

We spent more than an hour there before Flynn said we should go get me settled at his house. "Is the whole island this beautiful?" I asked as we drove away from the Crawfords.

"You get to decide that for yourself."

I couldn't wait to see more.

Chapter 19

We were on another tiny road with houses spread out about every quarter mile. The blacktop looked new and smooth. There was an openness that I hadn't seen before. Almost barren, but not like a desert or tundra. Grass was everywhere with just an occasional stand of trees. The sky felt so close. Most of the houses were simple with straight lines and little fanfare. The older ones were stone, often whitewashed. The newer ones had the same modest lines but the materials were different—siding or brick.

"I was hoping you'd see this," Flynn said, nodding at the road ahead of us. About a hundred feet away, coming around a bend in the road, was a man with a staff. To the sides and behind him were sheep. I couldn't see how many because of the bend in the road. "Come see."

We got out of the car and leaned on the hood, watching the man and his animals approach us. I heard a dog bark and saw it running along the side of the sheep and then turning to circle around behind them and up the other side.

"Hope you're not in a hurry, Flynn," the man said as he approached.

"Not at all. How are ya, James?"

"Couldn't be finer."

"This is my friend, Charlotte. From America."

"Pleased to meet ya, Charlotte." He tipped his hat.

"Thank you. You too. They're so cute."

"'Til they take a nip outta your hide," James said.

I jumped. "They bite?"

Flynn and James laughed. "No. They won't bother you at all."

James walked on Flynn's side of the car, and the sheep split almost down the middle. Soon we were surrounded by sheep.

"How many does he have?"

"A couple hundred right here," Flynn said. The dog scampered back and forth, keeping the sheep moving in the right direction. When they passed, we got back in the car and continued down the road.

Flynn pulled into a gravel driveway and parked the car by a small, whitewashed stone house. "This is home. That's Mum's house right there." He pointed at a house about a football field away. "Mum's planning on us for dinner if you're okay with that."

"Sure. I'm excited to meet her." That might have been overstating it just a little. I was still worried that she wouldn't like me because I was an American girl who might be interested in her son.

Flynn carried my bags to the house and I followed him. I was barely in the door and already I was glad I would be staying here. The house was small, cozy, and rustic, but most of all it was charming.

"Flynn, I love it."

"Not too primitive for you?"

I shook my head as I looked around. "No. You might have a hard time getting me out of here. Did you do all this?"

"It was a barn when I was growing up. The neighbor milked his cows right over there." He pointed at the kitchen. "It's closer to Mum's house than to theirs, so I asked if I could buy it from them. They took almost a year to decide but then they sold it to me and I changed up the inside."

"You're good at this. If you came back to the United States and did this to old barns, they'd put you on HGTV. Especially with your rugged good looks and your accent."

Flynn winked. "Let's not mention that in front of Mum."

I motioned like I was zipping my lips.

"Here's the bedroom. I put on clean sheets."

"That was kind of you."

"Come back here, and I'll show you the best part."

I remembered the stream and hill behind Flynn's house from the little tour he had given me on Skype, but that hadn't prepared me for the perfection that was his back yard. About forty feet from the house was a shallow stream. I could hear the water singing over the rocks from the back door. A stone fire pit with a few chairs arranged around it sat not far from the water. We walked across the short grass to the stream.

"If you walk about three miles that way, the stream will empty into the sea. If you walk a mile that way"—he pointed at the hill across the little bridge—"you'll have a view that way of the ocean and that way of Stornoway."

I knew before I went home I wanted to do both of those. I sighed. "I can't imagine anything in the world that would make you want to leave this."

Flynn looked back at his house. "It would take a lot."

I wiped my sweaty palms on my jeans as we walked down the little road to Flynn's childhood home. "Don't worry. She's a kind woman," he said and squeezed my shoulder.

"I'm sure she is."

I saw her standing in the doorway before we had even turned into the short driveway. "So you're Charlotte," she said, her arms spread wide.

"That's me. I'm happy to meet you, Mrs. Macgruger."

"Mary. Call me Mary."

Mary was a tall, stout woman. In America we would have said she had big bones, because stout would seem insulting. But here, in this place where the sky seemed to touch the earth and wind blew pink into everyone's cheeks, stout seemed like a compliment.

Mary's home was nice and tidy but seemed a little sterile and boring after Flynn's. The kitchen looked like a kit from the eighties. The carpeting was a pale teal that went out of style before most of it had been created in the factories, and the light fixtures were a dated, shiny brass. But it smelled like heaven.

"I hope you like lamb pie."

"If it's anything like the chicken pie I had in Glasgow, then I'll love it."

"Oh no. You already had meat pie?"

"Please don't feel bad. It was delicious."

"We've got lamb pie and raspberry cranachan for you and me. Plain cranachan for Flynn."

"You really should eat the raspberries. Chicken."

"I prefer it plain, if ya please."

"Well, I love raspberries, but what is cranachan?"

"It's like a trifle," Mary said.

"That sounds wonderful."

It was. The filling was savory and rich and the crust was perfect. "Is this pie crust a Scottish secret?" I asked. "I've made pie crust before, but it's never been like this."

"There might be a few tricks we know. I can teach ya if you want to learn."

"Now, Mum, she's not on vacation to cook."

I shook my head and spoke as soon as I had swallowed. "He's wrong. I would love to learn."

"And I'd love to teach."

"See, I told you she'd like you," Flynn said as we walked back to his house after dinner.

"She's very nice," I said. I was surprised how well I could see this late. I looked around for a moon and was amazed it was just a sliver. The stars were brilliant and lit the road almost as well as a larger moon would have. It was cold, and I pulled my sweater closer around me.

"I'll come in and start a fire for ya," Flynn said at the door. "And then I'll get out of your way so you can get some sleep."

"You should stay for a little while. Can we talk about our plans for the next several days? I want to be sure I get to fit in a few things."

I wrapped up in a blanket and sat cross-legged in the corner of a small, plaid sofa while Flynn built a fire. I pulled a notebook out of my purse and started a list of things I wanted to do. When the fire was roaring, Flynn scooted back and leaned against the front of the sofa, his legs stretched out in front of him, his arm resting in front of my legs.

"There's room for you up here," I said.

"I'm good. This is comfortable. So what have you got on your list so far?"

"Cooking with Mary."

"That's first on your list? I thought you came here to see me." Flynn's voice was teasing, and he smiled at me.

"Would you like to cook with us? I'm sure your mom wouldn't mind."

"Naw. I'll use that time to work at the Crawfords."

"Perfect."

"What else?"

"I want to help you with something at the Crawfords. I can hammer things or carry things to you or whatever."

"Do you want to help with the fireplace?"

"Really? You'll let me?"

"Aye. I need someone to carry all the rocks to me."

"Good."

Flynn brushed the back of his fingers up and down across my knee. "Charlotte, I was joking. You can help me with the fireplace, but I won't have you carry all the rocks."

"I don't care what I do. I just want to help. And I want to golf."

"We can do that."

"And I want to hike up to the view on the hill and I want to walk down the stream to the ocean."

"It sounds like you want to go home with the rosy cheeks of the Scottish and a face full of freckles."

"I like freckles," I said and reached out and touched the freckles on his cheek.

Startled at the warmth of his skin, I snatched my hand back and picked up the notebook. Flynn put his hand over mine. It was warm and a little rough. He left it there while he spoke. "You keep making your list and you can show it to me tomorrow. I'm going to go." He gently squeezed my hand and then stood and walked to the door. "I'm opening the store tomorrow. You can come with me if you want."

I stood by the couch but didn't move toward the door. "Maybe tomorrow morning would be a good day to walk up that mountain."

"Don't turn an ankle. If you're not back by the time I get home, I'll come looking for you."

"See you tomorrow," I said.

Flynn waved and closed the door behind him.

I walked to the window and watched him walk out of the driveway and toward his mom's, a tall silhouette that slowly disappeared into the darkness.

Chapter 20

I heard Flynn's car drive by while I dressed. After a quick inventory of the kitchen, I boiled two eggs and made a piece of toast with jam. I filled a little bag with raisins and nuts and tucked it in the pocket of my hoodie. I couldn't find any plastic water bottles, so I filled a mason jar with water. It was clunky and hard to hold, but I found a backpack in the closet.

A small bridge crossed the stream, not far from the fire pit. I stopped to listen to the water for a few minutes and then started up the hill.

From Flynn's backyard, the hill didn't look like much, but as I began to climb, I realized I had underestimated it. It was much steeper than it looked, and beneath the grass were a lot of rocks. Some were firmly in the ground, but I had to be careful not to twist my ankle on them. Others were loose and if I wasn't careful of my footing, they would slip out from under me. I almost fell twice before I slowed down and moved more cautiously.

The air was cold and a brisk breeze blew in my face. In spite of that, the exertion made me hot and soon I unzipped my hoodie.

Behind me, Flynn's house looked small. The next neighbor down the road had a large house with several outbuildings. This was probably the neighbor who had sold Flynn the barn. There were two cars parked next to the house and a tractor by the barn. They looked like toys from this distance.

I took a drink of my water and continued up the hill. It took longer than I had expected. I was sweaty and out of breath by the time I reached the top. I turned around and looked at the view. I could see all the way to Stornoway and the water beyond. I couldn't see Flynn's house anymore, because it was situated too close to the bottom of the hill, but when I looked the other direction, farms dotted the countryside all the way out to the ocean. A tractor worked in one field, another was spotted with cattle and others were just grass. From this distance, it looked like the grass was green water with waves rolling across its surface.

Large, black rocks spotted the ground. I found one with a smoother side and sat down, my back against the rock. Wind whipped my hair into my face, so I pulled out my ponytail, twisted my hair into a high bun, and secured it with the elastic.

I had no idea what time it was and I didn't want to look at my phone to find out. I just wanted to sit here, suspended in time and space. I rested my head on my knees and looked out at Stornoway. I had seen a similar view of the city when I had been planning my trip and had looked at the Isle of Lewis up close on Google Earth. This wasn't exactly the same, but it was close. The streets criss-crossed in an orderly way. Somewhere down there was Macgruger's Hardware. Flynn was probably still there, helping customers with their projects.

I couldn't help but compare this view of Stornoway with the views I'd seen of San Francisco. They both sat at the water's edge but they were so different. In a city of millions I hadn't found lasting love, but on this island of thousands, people had found their happily ever after. How did the right people find each other? Would Jessie find love again? She was pretty and happy and friendly. Was there someone here for her now that Bruce was gone?

Would I have better luck in a tiny place like this than I had among the millions in the bay area? And then like it did every time I'd had time to think in the last month, my mind wandered to Angus. I had felt angry every time I had thought about him, but sitting on top of this hill, I was having trouble mustering up any indignation at all. Instead, all I felt was sadness. I wasn't sure if the ache in my heart was because of the beauty in front of me or the chaos I had left at home. The ache moved up from my chest to my throat and finally to my eyes and I cried. I didn't wipe away the tears. I let the sun and the wind dry them on my cheeks.

I don't know how long I sat there. I had no desire to move. My body felt heavy and I imagined myself sprouting roots and staying on this hilltop forever. It was like I was shackled to the rock and the sun and wind were my guards.

I saw Flynn before I heard him. I knew I should shout

out and tell him I was sorry he'd had to come all this way looking for me, but instead I just watched him approach. He smiled as he got closer and I smiled back.

"It's hard to leave once you get up here, isn't it?" he said, lowering himself to sit beside me. I slid over a little, making room for him to lean against the rock. Our shoulders touched as we looked at the view, and for a moment, I wished things were different. It would be nice to snuggle in and let Flynn help me forget all I'd left behind, but I knew that wouldn't be fair.

"It's so peaceful up here."

Neither of us spoke for a couple of minutes. Finally Flynn pulled his knees up and rested his arms on them. "Want to tell me why you've been crying?"

I sighed and lifted my face toward the sun. "You can tell?"

Flynn laughed. "You've got salt streaks on your cheeks."

I tried to smile.

"I don't think this is about your ex who's getting married. This seems like a different kind of suffering than when I was there. And you kept telling me no when I'd ask you to come, and then suddenly you tell me you're coming. Something made you change your mind, and I think it's the same thing that's eating you up."

I glanced at Flynn and he was looking far away at the water. I wiped my eyes with the sleeve of my jacket.

"I won't lie," Flynn said. "At first I thought you were coming for me, and I was happy about it."

"I'm sorry Flynn."

"Naw, it's okay. Now I know you wanted to come

because you're broken inside."

And there it was. I was broken inside and either no one had noticed or they hadn't mentioned it because they didn't know what to do about it. But Flynn had noticed.

He lifted his arm around my back and pulled me into his arms. I stayed there for a long time. At first I cried, and then the ache started to dissolve and I imagined it blowing away in the wind.

"What happened?" Flynn asked.

I shifted so I was sitting cross-legged, facing him. And I told him about Angus. I pulled at a thread on my jeans as I told him about Aleena. I felt the twist begin again in my stomach. I didn't want to be the cause of pain for her. Flynn reached over and took my hand in his.

"What are you going to do?"

I shook my head. "Why didn't he tell me sooner?"

"Why didn't you tell him?"

I looked up at Flynn's face. "What do you mean?"

"Charlotte." He looked and sounded like he was cajoling an obstinate child. "You obviously love him."

"Of course I do. We've been friends for years."

Flynn cocked his head. "That's not the kind of love I'm talking about."

"I've never thought about Angus like that."

"Maybe not before he kissed you, but you have since then. That's why you're worried about Aleena. And that's why you're not going to fall in love with me."

I looked at Flynn's handsome face. "I'm so sorry. I shouldn't have used you like this."

"Aye, but ya should have. Because we're friends. And because I live here." He looked out at the water. "And if there's any place in the world where you can have the room you need to figure things out, this is it."

Descending the hill took just as long as climbing it had. The footing was so precarious that one wrong step would send you tumbling down the side of the mountain, so we took slow, careful steps.

At first we didn't talk. I was thinking about what Flynn had said. Was I in love with Angus? Had I been for a long time? I thought about what might have happened if I hadn't played match maker with Aleena and Angus. I wondered if Will was right and they wouldn't make it. Would that make me happy or sad? And then I wondered what I would do if they did break up. I couldn't let my mind go there.

I looked at Flynn who was several steps ahead of me. I wondered what he was thinking. He probably wished he had never invited me to Scotland. Maybe he regretted turning his house over to me. What if he wanted me to go home. Should I offer to leave?

"Careful right here . . ." Flynn said just as his feet slipped out from under him. His back wasn't far from the steep hill so he didn't have far to fall, but he slid several feet before he managed to dig in his heels and come to a stop.

"Flynn, are you okay?" I hurried toward him.

"Don't come too fast," he said, just as my feet slipped out from under me and I slid right by him. He reached out his hand to stop me but just managed to grasp the hood of my jacket. It didn't break my fall, but it did pull the jacket right off my arms.

I could feel rocks digging into my back, but when I rolled onto my side and saw Flynn ten feet above me, holding my empty jacket by the hood, something inside me let go and I started to laugh. I couldn't stop, and Flynn started laughing as he slid down the hill to me.

"Are you okay?" he asked through his laughter.

"I'm not sure. I think my back might be cut up." And then I snorted and Flynn laughed harder. When I had gained my composure, I asked, "What about you? Are you hurt?"

"I don't think so, but I think . . ." He put his hands between his legs. "Yep, I think I've split my breeks."

I giggled. "Breeks?"

"Trousers. Breeks. Pants. It doesn't matter what you call them. I've split mine."

We both burst out laughing again. "Dang, my back is really stinging."

"Here, let me look." I turned my back toward Flynn and he carefully lifted up the back of my shirt. "Aye, you're bleeding a bit." And then he started laughing again.

"You're terrible, laughing at my pain."

"I'm sorry, Charlotte. I know it's not funny."

"Except it is."

"We've got to stop laughing so we can get off this hill and get your back bandaged."

"Okay, no more laughing," I said, trying to contain myself.

Flynn managed to get on his feet and I did my best not to look at his pants. When he was standing solidly, he reached down and helped me up. We grinned at each other.

"Nothing like a near death experience to pull us out of the doldrums," Flynn said.

I couldn't help it. I started laughing again.

Somehow we made it off that hill, even though we laughed most of the way down. I couldn't remember when I had laughed so hard. It might have been when I was a child.

"Let's go to Mum's. I don't know if I have any bandages."

"What happened to you two," Mary said when we walked in the front door.

"We fell down the hill," Flynn said.

"You're a regular Jack and Jill, aren't ya?" Mary said, and we both started snickering.

"Mum, Charlotte's back needs some bandages," Flynn said.

"Come here. Let's take a look," Mary said.

"You should go change your pants," I said to Flynn.

"Oh dear, you've bled clear through your shirt," Mary said, and I snort-laughed again.

That night I couldn't sleep on my back. It was sore and stinging and I had ruined my shirt. But I felt happier than I had in ages.

Chapter 21

"The secret is using cold fat and not overworking your dough. See this? We want little pieces of cold fat that don't get kneaded in."

Mary had a fork and was putting quick work to the pie crust. "If it's too dry, add a little cold water, but don't let the fat melt in the flour."

I had spent most of the day at Mary's learning the art of pie crust. She had also shared her meat pie recipe and soon we would make a butterscotch pudding.

"Have you always lived in Stornoway?" I asked as Mary watched me roll out the first pie crust.

"I was born in Carloway, on the other side of the Isle. Calvin swept me off my feet and moved me all the way to Stornoway." Mary laughed. "And I've been here ever since."

"It's beautiful here. I've never seen anywhere like it."

"Aye, but it is. I still don't understand how a man can leave it." I knew she was talking about Bruce. "But I s'pose for some the pull of a woman can be stronger than the pull of the Isle." It seemed like she was talking to herself so I didn't interrupt. "But when the woman's gone, a man should come home."

Mary turned away from me and busied herself rinsing out a bowl. "Did you meet my Bruce?"

"Yes. He was very nice." Mary nodded. "It must have been hard when he left."

"Aye. It still is. But Flynn says he's made a place for himself and I s'pose I should be proud that a boy from a small place like Stornoway can rise to the top in a place like America." Mary wiped her eyes on her apron.

"You should come visit him."

"Naw. I'm an old woman. Bruce has come home every year and as long as he does that, I'll not be going so far away. No, no. Don't use the scraps again. That's what makes it tough." With one hand she brushed the used scraps into her other hand and threw them into a bowl. "For the chickens."

When we were finished baking, we cleaned the small kitchen together. "Flynn said you helped him build a fireplace."

"Aye, we built it yesterday." I laughed. "I just said 'aye' and I didn't even mean to."

Mary smiled. "The isle is growing on you."

"Aye, but it is." We laughed.

"Flynn's a big, strong man. Don't let him overwork you."

"Oh no, he didn't. I asked him if I could help and he didn't want me to carry the stones inside, so he taught me how to put in the cement and then build them up." I laughed again. "I'm probably saying it all wrong. Oh well. We finished the fireplace and it's beautiful. Want to see?"

I pulled out my phone and showed her the pictures I had taken when we finished our work.

"Aye. Very nice."

"I can't believe I only have three days left."

"The time has gone fast. I was afraid you'd grow bored of the Isle. It's not as exciting as the big city."

"This has been just what I needed."

On Sunday, we had taken Mary to the services in an old stone church. The pews were terribly uncomfortable and I could hardly understand what the minister was saying, but the music was pretty and Mary dabbed at her eyes as we sang. After church, we made sandwiches and followed the stream to the ocean and back. If Flynn was disappointed that we didn't have a romantic future together, he hid it well. He was kind and funny and filled the time with stories and games.

One morning, Mary had driven him to the hardware store so I could use his car and drive around the island. He seemed to sense that I needed some quiet time to learn how to be at peace with my thoughts. It seemed the island was trying to woo me because everywhere I went seemed more beautiful. Twice I waited for sheep to cross the road and both times I got out of the car and spoke to the shepherd.

I drove to Carloway before I knew Mary had grown up there. I wished I had known what house had been hers.

I ate by myself at a little restaurant called The Digby Chick. I couldn't understand the older man who took my order so I pointed at what I wanted on the menu. I ate a giant mushroom stuffed with onions and pears and cranberries. The Isle was not lacking in delicious food.

"I guess we're going to the fire tonight," I said.

Mary hmphed.

"Is there a reason for the fire? A celebration or something?"

"Naw. Just the bairns making mischief. We should get these in the oven so we can eat when Flynn gets home." I could tell she wanted to change the subject, so I didn't ask anything else about the fire.

We could see the fire from the road. The flames were at least as tall as Flynn, and already at least a couple dozen people mingled around the fire.

Flynn pulled his car off the blacktop and turned it off.

"They won't mind an American crashing the party?" I asked.

"No. You're not the first American to come," Flynn said. "Bruce met Kendra here."

I stopped. "Is that why your mom didn't want to talk about it?"

"Aye. It doesn't make sense, but she thinks this is to blame."

We started walking again, slowly making our way through the darkness to the fire. "Actually, it does make a little sense."

"It's easier to blame something like the fire instead of blaming Bruce."

"She's been so kind to me. I'm glad she doesn't blame all Americans."

A few people were roasting the biggest

marshmallows I had ever seen. Some drank beer while others drank sodas. A girl with frizzy, brown hair was playing a guitar and singing.

"Flynn, haven't seen you here in a while," said a man with a toddler on his shoulders.

"Been busy," Flynn said.

"I keep telling Jack we're getting too old for these," said a tall blonde walking beside him. "Never thought we'd come to these with our little hen." She pointed at the little girl on her husband's shoulders.

"Jessie thought I should bring my friend, Charlotte, so here we are."

I looked around and saw Jessie on the other side of the fire. She waved when she saw us.

"Flynn, we didn't have to come to this. I hate to upset your mom, especially if you didn't really want to come."

"Naw, no worries. This is the first time I've been this summer. I think Jessie was just using you as an excuse to get us here." He smiled.

"I'm glad you could come," said Jessie when we joined her.

"You want something to drink?" Flynn asked us.

"I'll take a Coke," Jessie said.

"That's fine," I said and Flynn left.

"He doesn't come much anymore," Jessie said. "I think it upsets his mum." I nodded. "I'm not sure why I come anymore. Everyone's getting so much younger." She laughed.

"Do you like it here?" I asked.

"At the fire?" She shrugged. "Sometimes."

I followed Jessie's gaze and saw Flynn standing by the

coolers. He was talking to the man with the toddler.

"I meant here in Stornoway," I said.

Jessie laughed and her dimples deepened. "Aye, this is the best place in the world."

"You've never wanted to move to Glasgow or somewhere else?"

She shook her head. "I was born right here in Stornoway and I'll probably die here. My family's lived here forever." She turned and looked at me. "Why d'ya ask?"

"I just wondered. I can see why you'd never want to leave. It's beautiful."

"Aye, it is."

I wanted to ask her about Bruce and if she would stay here even if it meant never falling in love again, but I didn't. I would be leaving soon and it was none of my business.

"She's good," I said, nodding at the girl with the guitar. She was playing a sad song that I didn't recognize.

"Aye. But have ya heard Flynn play?"

"Flynn plays the guitar?"

"Aye, and he's good. But when ya ask him, he always says no."

"Really? I want to hear this."

Jessie laughed. "Good luck. He's a stubborn one."

Suddenly I had an idea. "Let's have our own fire before I leave. At Flynn's. You could come and his mom and we can talk him into playing for us."

"I'll come, but I don't know if he'll play."

"We won't tell him until we're all there. Then we'll have him outnumbered."

Jessie giggled. "If anyone can make him do it, it's probably you." There was something wistful in Jessie's voice but I didn't have time to think about it because Flynn had returned. He sat down beside me and we listened to music and talked. After about an hour, Flynn started to seem restless.

"I'm a little tired," I said. "Do you mind if we go soon?"

"We can go now," he said.

"I'll leave now, too," said Jessie. "I'll walk up to the road with you."

We were quiet on the ride back to Flynn's house. The moon was a little larger and bathed the road in so much light, it almost seemed like we didn't need headlights.

When Flynn parked the car by his house, I reached for the handle to get out, but paused. "Are you okay?"

"I'm good."

"You seem a little quiet tonight."

Flynn sighed. "I don't like the fire. I'm too old for it. I don't know why Jessie likes it so much."

"Are you sure she does?"

"She's always asking me to come. It upsets mum."

"And it makes you a little sad, too?"

Flynn shrugged.

"You miss him, don't you?"

"I don't know."

"Tell me. You're always making me tell you everything."

Flynn smiled. "No I don't. I tell you what you're thinking."

"Okay, so you want me to tell you what you're

thinking?" I asked, suddenly feeling nervous.

"Do ya think you can?"

"I'll give it a try." I shifted in my seat so I was facing him. I took a deep breath and started. "Sometimes you miss him so much it hurts. Other times you're so mad at him for leaving that you want to punch him. You hate that he abandoned you, but you're a little proud of him for having the guts to move so far away. And sometimes you wish you could follow him, but you won't because you love it here and you love your mum so you'll stay and be the responsible son."

Flynn wasn't smiling anymore, and I couldn't tell how he was feeling.

"Not bad. Is there more?"

"Yeah. Sometimes you're lonely," I said quietly, "but you're not sure how to fix it, so you just work hard and stay busy." I stopped talking and the car was silent for several long seconds before I spoke again. "And that's all I can read."

Flynn's hands were on the steering wheel and he looked out over the fields behind his house. I put my hand on his arm. "I'm sorry, Flynn."

He didn't pull his arm away, but he reached for the door handle, so I moved my hand, and we got out of the car.

"It's pretty warm tonight. Do ya need a fire?"

"No, I'll be fine," I said.

"So golf tomorrow morning?"

"I'll be ready."

"Good night, Charlotte."

I took a step toward him. "Flynn?" And then I took

two more steps and put my arms around him. At first he just stood there, but then he pulled me close and hugged me tightly. We held each other for a long time and then Flynn stepped away.

"See ya in the morning."

"Stop laughing at me." I tried to sound stern, but it was hard to blame him for an occasional chuckle at my expense. I'm a terrible golfer. I had tried it a couple of times at home and was so bad I'd sworn I would never play again, but golf was invented in Scotland and it had seemed like a good idea to give it a try.

We were on the eleventh hole and I was losing badly. If the course hadn't been so beautiful, I would have suggested we give up and find something else to do, but everywhere I looked was a view worthy of a postcard—green, rolling hills, Stornoway Harbor, and a lovely white clubhouse—so we persevered.

"I'm sorry. But you do know the object of the game is to get the little white ball in the hole, right?"

I ignored him and walked to the long grass to look for my ball. I had to be careful where I stepped. We were sharing the course with a herd of sheep. I still wasn't sure if they were strays and needed to be gathered home or if they were on the course intentionally, but they created an entirely different kind of hazard that I'd never seen before. Instead of sand traps and ponds, we were faced with an additional hazard—sheep droppings. I had already stepped in one pile and didn't want to step in another.

"What do I do if I can't find it?" I asked, after I had searched for my ball for several minutes.

"You lose."

I laughed. "Like that'll be a surprise. But really, what should I do?"

Fortunately, we had only seen two other golfers today and they were probably finished with the course by now, because I was slow. In a real round of golf, I'm sure I would have incurred a time penalty.

Flynn joined me in the long grass. "I should have just walked along and watched you golf," I said.

"Then what would I have laughed at?"

"At least I'm providing you with some good entertainment."

We paced back and forth in the area we had seen the ball drop.

"Oh, steamin' jobbies. You might want a new ball." Flynn had bent over and was holding the grass back.

"What did you say?" I walked over to see what he was looking at.

"I said you might want a new ball."

"No. Before that."

Flynn looked up at me, squinting in the sunshine. "I said 'steamin' jobbies.'"

I leaned over and rested my hands on my knees, laughing. "Steamin' jobbies? What does that even mean?"

Flynn pointed at the ground. My ball sat in a giant mound of sheep poop. It wasn't perched on the pile, ready to be hit. It was half buried. There would be no hitting the ball without sending sheep doo doo flying all over. "I think you should take a stroke and drop a new ball."

"Yeah, I think I will. But what is 'steamin' jobbies?'"

Flynn stood straight and stepped back onto the shorter grass.

"I don't know. My dad used to say it. I guess it could mean a hot pile of that." He pointed at the mess my ball was in. "Dad said it when he was bealin."

"Bealin? Sometimes I swear you're not speaking English."

"Bealin is angry. Very angry."

I laughed. "Steamin' jobbies. I think I might have to use that at home."

Flynn smiled. "It'll be like takin' a piece of Scotland home with ya."

Chapter 22

I t was my last night in Scotland and the Isle of Lewis had bestowed upon me a perfect night. The sky was clear and bright. The moon and the stars, like precocious children, clamored for attention.

We sat around the fire pit in Flynn's back yard. Mary and Jessie had joined us for the giant marshmallows. The creek softly bubbled in the background.

"Are ya happy to get home?" Mary asked.

I shrugged. "It'll be nice to see my family, and I have a project I'm excited about at work, but I have some hard things I have to take care of, and I still don't know what I'm going to do."

"You'll figure it out," Flynn said.

"This has been the best vacation of my life."

"Maybe you should stay a while longer," Jessie said.

I laughed. "I think Flynn might want his house back."

"You can stay in my house as long as ya want, but the hard things won't go away just 'cause you're here."

"I know."

"It's been a pleasure having you here," Mary said.

"You're just like a Scottish lass."

I knew that was a huge compliment coming from a woman who had every reason to resent American girls. "Thank you. And I'll be able to cook like one when I get home, thanks to you."

Jessie cleared her throat and I knew it was time. "I'll be right back," I said.

I walked to Flynn's house and retrieved the guitar I had found in his closet. I had used a guitar tuner I'd found in his case to try to tune it. It sounded okay to me, but only someone who played a guitar would know for sure. I carefully carried it out to the fire and sat down.

"You play the guitar?" Mary asked.

"No. But I heard Flynn does."

Flynn shook his head. "No, no, no."

"It's my last night here, Flynn. Please play a song or two."

Flynn looked back and forth between Mary and Jessie. "It wasn't me," Mary said, putting her hands up in surrender. Jessie just smiled.

"I'm not any good. Let's just enjoy the sound of the water."

"Someone's going to play a song tonight. I'll just start playing until you're ready to take your turn." I grinned at him and settled the guitar on my lap. I wasn't sure if I was holding it right, but I pretended I knew what I was doing.

And then I started strumming and holding down random fingers. The sound was abrasive and unpleasant. "You are my sunshine, my only sunshine." I continued singing and playing, even though the two actions had nothing to do with each other. I sang as much as I knew and then paused. "Should I keep going or do you want a turn?"

Flynn shook his head.

"You are my sunshine . . ." I began again.

"Fine, I'll do it."

Everyone laughed.

Flynn started playing, his fingers moving easily over the strings. I was surprised at how good it sounded. And then he started singing about a lass with sad, brown eyes and I felt like a balloon was being inflated bigger and bigger inside my chest and might pop right out at any moment. Flynn's voice was rich and mellow and the song was so melancholy.

"Wow," I said when he finished.

"I told you he was good," Jessie said, and Flynn gave her a good-natured glare.

"Consider that your going away present," Flynn said.

"Thank you. Can I have one more?"

"I don't know very many songs without music."

"Just one more?"

Flynn started strumming again. This song was happier. It was a song about lovely Stornoway. After a couple of lines, the others joined in, first Mary and then Jessie. I wished I knew the song and could sing along. I certainly agreed with the lyrics. When the song was over, Flynn leaned the guitar against his chair and sat back.

"Thank you." I knew he had just shared something he usually kept to himself. Flynn smiled at me and if Mary and Jessie hadn't been there, I would have had to hug him.

"I'm tired. I think it's time for me to go to bed." Mary pushed herself out of her chair.

"I'll walk you home, Mum."

"Be sure to stop by in the morning and say goodbye," Mary said.

"I will."

Mary put her arm through Flynn's and they left.

"I'm glad you told me he could play," I said to Jessie when Flynn and Mary were too far away to hear.

"He must really like ya," Jessie said. "He doesn't play for people very often. A couple of times when I've brought something by the house, I've heard him playing, but that's just for himself. Once I stood by the door and listened to three or four songs before I knocked."

"You have a lovely voice, too," I said.

"Naw," Jessie said and waved me off. "I think I'll go home now. Ya don't need a tag-along on your last night here." I wanted to assure her Flynn and I were just friends and she could stay, but I had a couple of things I wanted to talk to him about, so I didn't discourage her from leaving.

"It was wonderful meeting you," I said, standing to give her a hug.

"You too. Maybe you'll come back some time."

"I don't know. This has been amazing, but it might have been a once-in-a-lifetime thing for me."

Jessie hugged me back and then walked to her car and left.

I sat alone for several minutes. The flames had died to embers but I didn't want to go inside yet, so I threw on a couple more pieces of wood and it crackled back to life. I looked at the back of Flynn's house and felt a surprising twinge of sadness. How strange to feel homesick for a place that had never been home.

"Where's Jessie?" Flynn asked.

"She went home."

"You warm enough?"

"Yes. It feels good."

Flynn slid his chair a little closer to mine and sat down.

"I'm sorry you're leaving."

"Me too. This has been perfect. You've all been so kind and generous. Thank you."

Flynn nodded. We watched the fire for several moments and then he spoke. "Have you decided what you're going to do when you get home? About Angus?"

I sighed. "I don't want to hurt Aleena."

"Do you want to hear what I think about it?"

"Of course."

"If you and Angus love each other, Aleena will get over it." I cringed a little. I still wasn't used to thinking about me and Angus loving each other. "But if you don't tell him how you feel, and he marries her even though he loves you . . . If she ever finds out, that will be much harder for her to get over."

I nodded. "This is so hard."

"Do you love him?"

"I don't know."

"Charlotte."

"I guess I do."

Flynn leaned toward me and put his hand on my arm. "You've suffered enough. You've watched a lot of men leave and go on to find happiness. I know you're worried about your friend. That shows what kind of person you are. But you deserve to be happy, too. You need to tell the truth."

"I know." And I did know. I wasn't sure how I was going to do it, but this last nine days on this beautiful island, with time to think and laugh and find peace, had convinced me that I had to be honest, no matter how hard it was.

I turned in my chair and took Flynn's hand in both of mine. "And now I need to tell you the truth."

Flynn raised his eyebrows. I smiled at his confused expression. He looked so lovely in the firelight that I felt a pang of sadness that I wouldn't fall in love with him, that I would probably never come back to this heavenly place. "Flynn, you deserve to be happy, too. You deserve to be loved. I don't want you to be lonely."

"I'll be fine."

"I want you to do something for me."

"I'm not marrying you, Charlotte, no matter how much you beg me."

"You're breaking my heart."

"You'll get over it, I'm sure."

I smiled at him. "I want you to take Jessie to dinner. On a date."

Flynn laughed and tried to pull his hand away, but I held it tightly. When I didn't laugh, he got quiet. "She's in love with Bruce." I shook my head. "She's loved him since before he went to school."

"Bruce has been gone a long time. I know he left a hole here for all of you. But you're here. And so is Jessie."

"So you think she should settle for me?"

"Oh, Flynn. Whoever ends up with you will not be

settling." Flynn looked at our hands. "Please. Promise me you'll take her out to a nice dinner."

"You're really desperate to keep that husband maker record going, aren't you?" The side of Flynn's mouth was quirked up, so I knew he was teasing.

"You don't want to be my one failure, do you?"

"I'll take her to dinner."

"Make sure she knows it's a date. A real date. Okay?"

"Okay."

"Promise?"

"I promise." I let go of his hand and sat back in my chair, satisfied.

The fire died down and eventually we walked to the house. Flynn put his guitar away and then we stood at the door. "I'm glad ya came, Charlotte. Even though things didn't turn out like I'd hoped, I'm glad ya came."

"So am I. You'll never know how much this meant to me." I reached up and put my hand on his cheek. "You are the very best kind of man."

Flynn took my hand from his cheek and kissed my palm before he turned and walked out of his house.

Chapter 23

*M*om and Dad picked me up at the airport. Mom hugged me tightly before she pulled back and looked at me intently.

"How was your trip?" Oh, Mom. In spite of the ordinariness of the question, I could tell she was really asking, "Are you in love with Flynn? Are you moving to the other side of the world? Are we losing our daughter?"

"My trip was wonderful, but I'm not moving to Scotland."

Mom let out a quick breath, like someone had punched her in the stomach. "Really? Things didn't work out?"

I shook my head. "Flynn will forever be a dear friend, but that's all."

"I'm sorry, dear." Now that she knew I wouldn't be moving to Scotland, she could be generous in her condolences.

"It's okay. I'm so glad I went. I wish you could see the Isle of Lewis. I've never seen anything like it and this was exactly what I needed."

After Stornoway, I found San Francisco too big, too loud, too crowded. It felt both familiar and disquieting. I reminded myself that this was home. I knew that after a few days I would adjust to the commotion and the pace and that made me a little sad.

"What have I missed?" I asked from the back seat.

"Will and Gina's living room is finished," Mom said. "They even got new furniture. You'll have to go see it once you're settled back in. They did a great job."

"And Emily just keeps growing," Dad said.

"I need to get over there before she's walking."

Grandpa Guo was sitting outside his shoe repair shop, holding his laptop. "Charlotte, where have you been? I haven't seen you for days."

"I took a trip to Scotland."

"Oh, so far away. I thought maybe you'd moved."

"Nope. I'm still here."

"Good, good. I thought you'd moved and Mia's man would move in."

I thought about what he had said as we climbed the stairs and then it came to me. Had Graham called Mia? I was disappointed she wouldn't be home from work for a couple more hours. It seemed we had some things to catch up on.

"Come out to dinner as soon as you're over the jetlag," Mom said. "You can show us your pictures and tell us all about your trip."

I was tired, but I wanted to be sure I saw Mia when she got home, so I snuggled in with a blanket on the couch. I fell asleep almost immediately.

"Shhh. Don't wake her. She's probably exhausted."

"Maybe we should go out to dinner and let her sleep."

"Just let me change real quick."

It took me a minute to realize I was hearing voices and not dreaming. When I opened my eyes, Graham was standing in the doorway of the kitchen, his back to me. I pulled myself to a sitting position and rubbed the sleep out of my eyes.

"Graham?"

Graham turned to face me. "Sorry, did we wake you?"

"That's okay. What's going on?" I pulled my feet up under me.

"We're just going to get some dinner. As soon as Mia changes."

"No. I mean what's going on?" I motioned back and forth between Graham and Mia's bedroom.

Graham smiled and stepped over to the couch. "I'll let Mia tell you." Then he lowered his voice. "But just so you know, I haven't told her I saw you in Philadelphia."

"Oh. So I shouldn't say anything?"

Graham shrugged. "That's up to you."

"Hey, you're awake."

"Yeah. Sort of."

"Welcome home." Mia came to the couch and leaned over to give me a hug. "It seems like you've been gone forever. Two weeks is too long."

I sighed. "I don't know. I think I could have stayed another week or two pretty easily."

"That good, huh? I want to hear all about it."

"It's not what you think."

"No Scottish boyfriend?"

I shook my head.

"Ah, I'm sorry. I was hoping you would come home in love."

Funny. I think I did come home in love. It just wasn't what everyone would expect. "It's okay. I had a great time, and the whole trip gave me some much-needed perspective."

"Good. If you're happy about it, then so am I." She stood in front of me, her hands on her hips, smiling. "Do you want to come to dinner with us?"

"No thanks. I'm too tired. I'd probably end up face down in my food."

Mia smiled at me. "Would you like us to bring back something for you?"

"I don't know. Where are you going?" I glanced over at Graham, and he was smiling too. They exchanged a look and then continued to smile at me.

"We were going to Mosso's. Do you want some lasagna?"

"Sure. That sounds good." I looked back and forth at them again. "Okay, what's going on?"

"Nothing," Mia said, swinging her hips a little, her hands still on them.

And then I saw it. "No way. No way. Are you serious?" I looked back at Graham, and he was nodding, a huge smile on his face. I looked back at Mia and she was beaming.

"We're engaged."

"Graham. Good work. Seriously."

"Thanks. I went to see my brother and his family and had an epiphany. I decided I'd better snag her before someone else did."

I stood and hugged Mia. "Congratulations. I'm so excited for you."

"Me too. I knew he'd come around eventually."

Graham stood and hugged me, too. "Thank you," he whispered.

"Any time."

"Welcome home, Charlotte," Will said as soon as I answered the phone. I leaned back to talk, glad for the break. It was my first day back at work and it had seemed interminable.

"It's good to be home. Mostly."

"Fun trip?"

"Truly amazing, Will. It's like I just spent two weeks in heaven. It was so beautiful and the people were so nice. And I learned how to cook some amazing things. I'm thinking I should invite the family to Mom and Dad's and I'll do the cooking."

"You name the time and we'll be there. By the way, have you talked to Angus or Aleena since you got home?"

"No. It feels like all I've done is sleep. I can't seem to get caught up. Why?"

"I'm sure it's nothing."

"What's nothing?" I sat up a little straighter. I should have talked to them when I got home, but knowing what

I had to do, as soon as I psyched myself up, made it hard to call them. I didn't want to be fake.

"It's just that I haven't talked to him since before you left. I could tell something was on his mind, but when I asked, he said he was just weighing some options for his future. I figured he was about to dump Aleena. Sorry. I know she's your friend. I just know how hard it is for Angus to move on past a certain point and I figured he was about there."

"When did you try him last?"

"Last night. Maybe he was at work. It's just that we never go this long without talking, so I was just hoping you'd heard from him."

"I haven't. But I'll try him. I'll try Aleena too."

"Great. Let me know if you talk to him, okay? I know he's got a lot going on. I just don't like not being able to reach him."

I tried Aleena after Will and I said goodbye, but her phone rang once and then went to voicemail, so I tried the restaurant.

"Is this Mr. Li?"

"Yes."

"Hi, this is Charlotte."

"Hm." It was part huff, part grunt, and completely unfriendly. I was taken aback. Mr. Li had always liked me. My hands were suddenly clammy, and I felt a little sick to my stomach.

"Is Aleena there?"

"She might be. Why do you want her?"

"I just wanted to talk to her. I've been out of town and . . ." I felt compelled to give him more information. It was almost like I was sticking up for myself, even though no one had attacked me. Yet. "Well, I'd just like to talk to her."

"She might be busy."

"Oh. Okay. I guess I'll try back. Or maybe I'll stop by later."

"You should call first." I wanted to cry, but there were no tears. All I could muster was a lump in my throat. Should I try Angus? Would he tell me what was wrong with Aleena? I looked at the clock on the phone. It was after four. I was glad to be almost finished with this eternal day. Who cared about cheesy souvenirs when you wanted to remember The Isle of Lewis? Okay, I cared. But it still didn't keep my mind tethered to San Francisco and my office.

Call me a coward, but I just wasn't ready to face Angus yet—either in person or on the phone—so I texted Aleena instead.

Me: Hey, is something wrong? Your dad's screening your calls and I didn't make the cut. Give me a call when you've got a minute.

Aleena: He's just worried about me.

Me: Is something wrong?

Aleena: I'm sure Angus has filled you in on all the fun details.

Me: I haven't talked to Angus since I got back. What fun details are you talking about?

Aleena: Really, Charlotte? If you weren't interested in Angus, that's fine. But I never imagined you'd try to use me to distract him for you. You could have told me what you were doing. At least then I would have known things wouldn't work out.

Me: That's not how it happened. We really need to talk. Please.

Aleena: I'm not ready to talk about it and I don't know when I will be.

Me: I would really like to explain a few things.

Aleena: I'm sure you would. Hey, at least you don't have to worry about finding someone else to occupy his time. He probably won't be bugging you from Kansas City.

Kansas City? What was she talking about? Dread dropped into my stomach and lodged itself there like a stone. I wanted to talk to Aleena and make things right with her.

But I had to talk to Angus.

Chapter 24

I only had forty-five more minutes of work. I couldn't cut out early after being gone for two weeks, so I would endure it.

Even though she didn't want to talk to me, I couldn't leave Aleena hanging, so I sent her one final text.

Me: Aleena, whatever happened, I'm sorry you're upset. I promise I wasn't setting you up to distract Angus. I love both of you and thought you'd be a good match. There are things I really want to talk to you about. Please call me in the next couple of days. If you don't, I'll be calling you. And I'll keep calling until we can talk. I hate that you think I would set you up to be hurt. I promise I'd never do that.

Aleena didn't respond, and at exactly five o'clock, I closed my office door and left.

I was in such a hurry to leave work that I didn't fully formulate a plan. I sat in my car in the parking garage and tried to gather my thoughts. I could call and tell Angus I wanted to see him, but I feared he might respond to a phone call the same way Aleena had, and then I would be stuck.

It seemed obvious that Will didn't know anything about Kansas City or he would have said something when he called. It didn't seem that Angus had confided in Will, which was almost unheard of. They had talked about everything since they were boys.

I could call Angus's parents, but even though that might be easier, it would look like I was going behind his back. I needed to face this squarely and find out what was going on.

And then a feeling of peace came over me and I felt as calm as I had sitting on the hill above Tolsta Beach on the Isle of Lewis. I had sat on that grassy slope and watched the waves crash onto the white sand beach, colliding with the tall, black rocks that rose out of the sand. It was a beautiful place, and it was there that I had determined I would tell Angus I thought he was right, that there was something between us. I wanted to tell him what I had discovered in my heart.

I turned the key in the ignition and backed out of my parking place. I needed to see him. I didn't know what was going on with Kansas City, and even though I felt terrible about Aleena being hurt, I suddenly realized what that meant. Angus was free. All I had to do was let him know how I felt and everything would be okay.

It took me more than an hour to get to Angus's apartment, but I didn't curse the traffic. It didn't aggravate me at all. It gave me time to think, and the more I thought, the more I was ready to throw my arms around Angus's neck and repeat The Kiss.

I couldn't remember the day we first met. He was just suddenly part of our lives—coming home after school several nights a week, playing games, riding bikes, and watching *Jeopardy*. Angus had always known more of the right answers. Will and I thought he should apply to go on the show. I had even sent in a letter to Alex Trebek, telling him Angus would make a great contestant, but Alex never responded.

The closer I got to Angus's apartment, the more excited I became. Lucy said Paul thought about the kiss and asked Ivy to dinner. Maybe in honor of Lucy, I should take Angus out to dinner and then at the end of the night, we could share another kiss. But this one would be better, because I wouldn't feel guilty that he was dating Aleena and that she was right there in the backyard.

Yeah, right. No way did I want to wait until the end of the evening. Maybe I should just kiss him as soon as he opened the door. There would be very little I would need to say after that.

My heart rate started going wild as I turned the corner onto Angus's street. Fate was smiling on me. There was a parking place less than a block from his apartment. I parked and started down the sidewalk. I put my hand on my chest, trying to settle the rapid heart rate. I laughed a little as I thought about what it would sound like through a stethoscope. Maybe that's how I should tell Angus I love him.

"Hey Angus, grab your stethoscope and listen to my heart. Can you figure out what it's saying?"

Oh. My. Cheesy. What was wrong with me? Did orthopedists even use stethoscopes?

The kiss would be much better. And much less cheesy.

I knocked. Loud music came from the apartment next door. It was a rap song with lyrics that made me cringe. This wasn't exactly the best soundtrack for a perfect kiss.

I was about to knock again when Angus appeared at the tall, narrow window beside the door. I couldn't be sure because there was glass between us, but it looked like he sighed. I smiled and gave a little wave. He didn't smile back.

My excitement faltered a bit.

Angus opened the door and moved aside so I could enter.

I stepped into the little hallway. Angus closed the door and started walking toward the living room, so I followed. He sat in a chair. When he didn't say anything, I sat in the corner of the couch.

"Hi, Angus."

"Welcome back from Scotland." The words were friendly, but the tone wasn't.

"Yeah, I got back a couple of days ago." Angus nodded. "The jetlag has been atrocious."

"I'll bet."

He wasn't making this easy for me. Not that he should. I hadn't made it easy for him.

"How are you?" I asked. Now that I was here, the idea of planting a gigantic, life-changing kiss on him seemed ludicrous. My body must have been momentarily overtaken by the star of a romantic comedy or a music video, because I would never have the confidence to be so bold.

"Um . . ." I rubbed my hands up and down my thighs.

I wasn't sure whether to start with Aleena, or Kansas City, or I love you.

"What is it, Charlotte?"

I took a deep breath. "You and Aleena broke up?"

"I suppose she told you."

"Not exactly. She won't talk to me."

"She took it pretty hard."

I nodded. She had been falling in love with Angus. Of course she had taken it hard. "I really thought you two would be good together."

"It isn't her fault. She's great. I should never have let you set us up."

"Angus. What's going on with Kansas City?"

For a second, Angus looked stunned, but a moment later his face was back to its stony expression. "Dr. Fickland recommended me for a hip fellowship in Kansas City. So I'll be heading there in August."

Hulk Hogan might as well have body slammed me to the floor. "What about your residency? I thought you'd be here a few more years."

"It's unusual, but Dr. Fickland is friends with a doctor out there, and when he heard about the fellowship, he thought it was a good fit for me. They worked things out, so I'll be finishing my residency there along with the hip fellowship."

I didn't even know what a hip fellowship was. I should have been more involved in Angus's life. I should have known about this. I should have been someone he talked to while he made his decision.

Angus laughed a short, humorless laugh. "Don't look so shocked, Chuck."

I took a deep breath and held it for a few seconds. "It's just that . . . I don't want you to go."

"You'll be fine. You don't need me here. Have Will and Gina go with you to therapy."

I could hardly get my words out, and I'm sure they sounded weak and strangled. "I don't think I'll need therapy again."

Now it was Angus's turn to look surprised, but then he smiled. Sort of. It didn't reach his eyes. "Congratulations."

"What?"

"Does this mean you're moving to Scotland, or did you convince him to come here?" He thought Flynn and I were together.

I shook my head. "That's not what I meant." Angus's face became a question. "Flynn and I are just friends."

The corner of Angus's mouth rose in a smile. "You're good at that, aren't you?"

"I'm good at what?" It wasn't easy keeping my voice steady, but I did.

"You're good at putting people who care about you in the friend zone."

"Angus." So much for romance and kisses.

The bass of the rap music pounded against the walls, a muted, but maddening thrum.

"Think about it," Angus continued. "There's me and Flynn, and maybe even Kyle. It was you that decided that wouldn't work, right?"

"Stop it, Angus." Nothing was ideal—Angus's chilliness and the neighbor's awful noise—but I knew I had to say what I had come to say, and the longer I waited, the harder it would be.

"I've spent the last few weeks thinking and figuring things out, and—" I sighed. "I came over here to tell you that I love you."

We looked at each other for several seconds. I couldn't tell what he was thinking, and I felt panic rising like a tsunami.

Angus was the first to look away. He rested his elbows on his knees and clasped his hands behind his neck. I couldn't see his expression, but everything about his body looked tight and on edge.

"Sorry, Charles. It's too late." His voice was low and filled with emotion.

"It can't be too late. It hasn't even been two months. Your feelings couldn't have changed that quickly. You said you love me. You broke up with Aleena. You should give us a chance." Desperation made my mouth run wild, but the entire time I spoke, Angus slowly shook his head, and I finally stopped.

Angus sat back up and looked at me with pain-filled eyes. "Charlotte, I don't think I have any more chances left to give. I've been waiting for you for years. I'm moving on."

"But . . ." I wanted to remind him that I hadn't known how he felt.

"Please let me finish. Every time you've broken up with someone, I've planned how I'm going to tell you. But I've never wanted to be a rebound guy or the one you settle for because you're sad. So I've waited for you to be okay and then, before I can tell you how I feel, you're dating someone else. I know it's because you're hopeful and optimistic. That's one of the things I've always admired about you, but it's been years now and I don't think I can do it anymore.

"I told myself it was the last straw when you set me up with Aleena. I knew then that there was no hope for us. If you had any interest in me at all, you wouldn't be trying to be my match maker."

"But, The Kiss. What about that?"

"That was a mistake."

"Don't say that."

"Something about being there for your birthday made me think I should try one last time to see if there was anything there. I wanted to know for sure before I said yes to the fellowship. You gave me my answer."

"No, Angus." I felt like crying. "You should tell them no. You should stay here."

"I can't. It's done. I won't have a position here. I have to go."

"But I didn't know. You never said anything about how you feel about me."

"Come on, Charlotte. I think everyone had it figured out but you."

Had everyone known? Will was the only one who had ever mentioned it. Then I remembered Kyle saying Wyatt had thought Angus and I would be dating. At the time, it had seemed like a joke, but maybe she was just a lot smarter than I am.

"I'm sorry. I was so stunned when you kissed me. I didn't know what to do, and all I could think about was not hurting Aleena."

"I wish you'd have cared as much about not

hurting me."

Ouch. There was nothing to say to that. I had been so blind.

I leaned forward on the couch and put my hand on Angus's arm. "I'm so sorry. I didn't know how you felt. I didn't realize how I felt either. But I know now."

Angus stood, pulling his arm out from under my hand. "I have to be at the hospital early tomorrow, and I've got a few things I still need to get done tonight."

It took me a dazed minute before I gathered my thoughts and stood. I needed to kiss him, break this terrible spell. The thumping music became louder as Angus opened the door.

I stopped at the door and faced him. The sorrow in his eyes squeezed my wildly hammering heart. I had put that sadness there. My pulse pounded in my ears like waves crashing into rocks. I put my arms around his waist and hugged him. His arms didn't move. I was terrified, but desperate to let him know I was here and I loved him. I stood on my tiptoes and touched his lips with mine.

For a moment, he didn't move, and I thought he might respond, but then he turned his face so my lips were on his cheek. Embarrassed, I fell back to my heels.

"Charlotte, please don't make things harder than they already are."

I took a step back, rejected and disappointed.

"When do you leave?"

"August."

I nodded. "Can we get dinner or something before you go?"

Angus sighed, and I saw a slight crack in his resolve.

"I don't know, Chuck."

"Angus, we've been friends for years." A tear that I hadn't even realized I was shedding slipped down my cheek. I quickly brushed it away.

"Sure, we can have dinner."

I felt like screaming at the occupants of the next-door apartment, but instead I turned and walked away.

I glanced back. The music had drowned out the sound of the door closing. Angus was gone.

This had not gone according to plan.

There had to be a way to convince Angus that he should give me another chance. His feelings couldn't have changed that quickly. He could call the doctor who had arranged the fellowship and tell him he had changed his mind. He could convince them to let him stay.

I needed to think. I needed to figure things out. I had won Angus's heart without even knowing it and now I'd lost it. Whatever it took, I had to win it again.

I needed to come up with a new plan.

Coming in February, 2015

The final book in The Husband Maker Series

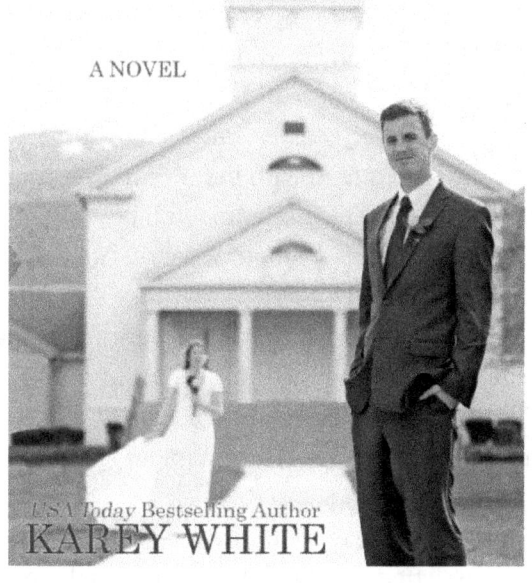

THE
Wife
MAKER

A NOVEL

USA *Today* Bestselling Author
KAREY WHITE

Author's Message

Thank you so much for picking up and reading my book. With so many reading options out there, I want you to know I'm honored. I hope you enjoyed entering Charlotte's roller-coaster world and I hope you enjoyed traveling to Scotland with her. I think we should all go to Stornoway together sometime. It'll be a blast! We can eat good food and talk about books—two of my favorite things to do.

As an author, my greatest desire is to have happy readers who spread the word about my books. If you'd be willing, I'd be so grateful for a review on Goodreads or Amazon or wherever else you might share your thoughts on books.

If you'd like to be notified of new releases, sign up for my newsletter in the right column at kareywhite.com. While you're there, feel free to send me a message. I love to hear from readers!

Happy Reading!
Karey

Acknowledgements

While I might be the one that gets the words out of my head and onto the page, there are so many people who help make it happen. For their contributions, I'm so grateful.

First, I want to thank my Father in Heaven for too many things to count. It's because of Him that my life is so rich and challenging and rewarding.

Thank you to Savannah, Dad and Mom, and Lori, for being my chapter-by-chapter readers. When I know that I'll have you asking for more at the end of the day, it keeps me moving. Thank you to Rachael, who helped me with plotting, brainstorming, and commas. You always help me fill in the gaps. So glad we're friends. Thank you to Leslie, Stephanie, Corinne, and Kathy, my beta readers. I'm so grateful for your honesty and encouragement. The book is better because of you. A special thanks to my friend, Missy, for her Scottish expertise. I can't tell you how happy I am that you lived on the Isle of Lewis. I must confess to a few feelings of jealousy.

Thanks to Dale and Renae, for letting me get away to

write at their lovely cabin, a quiet place where the only distractions were the beautiful changing colors of fall and an alarm repair man who will definitely be making an appearance in an upcoming book.

Thanks to Leslie, Michaela, Hannah, Connor and Rachael for your help with the cover. I love it.

Thank you to my four amazing children for motivating me and pitching in. I couldn't love you more.

A huge thank you to Travis, for taking over most of the laundry, for putting up with my self-imposed deadlines, and for repeating what you've said when I've been plotting in my head instead of paying attention. I'm glad you were my match. I love you.

About the Author

Karey grew up in Idaho, Oregon, Missouri and Utah. Through the years, she's been a student, a teacher, a secretary, a clothing designer and seamstress, a wedding cake maker, a crafter, a scrapbooker, a cook, a housekeeper (alright, this skill she's still working on) a homework helper (until they pass her in math, somewhere around the third grade), and a calm and ladylike fan at her children's sporting events.

Nothing makes her happier than being with family and friends, eating good food and sharing good conversation and a few laughs. When she's with witty and clever people, she could stay there for hours. She loves to travel and see new places. Someday she hopes to take research trips to Norway, Iceland, Scotland, Denmark (while the tulips are in bloom), China, and New Zealand.

She and her husband are the parents of four children that make them look good. She loves salmon and marzipan (not necessarily together) and getting letters. Find out more about Karey and her books at kareywhite.com

If you enjoyed The Match Maker, you'll enjoy the
Meet Your Match series by Rachael Anderson.